THE SEMINOLE TRAIL

THE
SEMINOLE
TRAIL

DEE DUNSING

Illustrated by LARRY TOSCHIK

LONGMANS, GREEN AND CO.

NEW YORK · LONDON · TORONTO

LONGMANS, GREEN AND CO., INC.
55 FIFTH AVENUE, NEW YORK 3

LONGMANS, GREEN AND CO., LTD.
6 & 7 CLIFFORD STREET, LONDON W 1

LONGMANS, GREEN AND CO.
20 CRANFIELD ROAD, TORONTO 16

THE SEMINOLE TRAIL

PUBLISHED SIMULTANEOUSLY IN THE DOMINION OF CANADA BY
LONGMANS, GREEN AND CO., TORONTO

FIRST EDITION

LIBRARY OF CONGRESS CATALOG CARD NUMBER 56–9215

Printed in the United States of America

This book is affectionately
dedicated to my long-time friends
CONSTANCE GRAHAM HENDRICKS
GWEN GRAHAM YOUNGBLOOD AND
MARY McEWEN TOMPKINS.

Many Thanks

I HEREBY THANK Marjory Stoneman Douglas and Rinehart and Company for permission to quote from *The Everglades: River of Grass* and the University of Florida Press for the quotation from *Journey Into Wilderness*, written in the Seminole War years by Jacob R. Motte and edited in 1953 by James F. Sunderman.

Special thanks are due Harriet Emerson Cull and Laura Emerson Gradick of Jacksonville, Florida, for their opinions and criticism.

DEE DUNSING

Contents

CHAPTER		PAGE
1	THE SILVER CHEST	1
2	WAHOO SWAMP	17
3	CAPITULATION	33
4	VENGEANCE	46
5	FREE	58
6	THE BRIBE	66
7	COCKROACH KEY	76
8	THE FLY-UP-THE CREEK	87
9	SHAKOCHEE'S GIFT	98
10	ST. AUGUSTINE	106
11	SLOWLY THE TIDE TURNS	120
12	THE STRANGER	133
13	RETURN TO THE FOREST	142
14	THE SEARCH	152
15	CONFISCATED	168
16	PHANTOM ENEMY	177
17	THE BATTLE	186
18	WORK OF THE ROOT	197
19	GOING HOME	207

THE SEMINOLE TRAIL

Chapter 1

The Silver Chest

"The quail pipe and their new-hatched young run
like mice with their small cheeping, at the edge of
such pineland, and the brown marsh rabbit, with small
ears and no apparent tail, nibbles some bit of leaf."
—Marjory Stoneman Douglas
in *The Everglades: River of Grass*

IT WAS November—midafternoon and warm—when
Rod Wheeler discovered the footprints.

For three days he had been hunting them, first in the
country directly south of Lake George and Fort Volusia,
then in a wider circle that took him past a wrecked sugar
mill and abandoned fields which once had been planted
with corn, sugar cane and indigo.

Although Indians must have destroyed the mill, Rod
had not sighted any warriors, or signs of them. Until now.

Where the trail crossed another, he set his long Ken-
tucky rifle against a pine, took off his coonskin cap, and
wiped the sweat from his forehead. He was thinking a
wash-up in the next spring would feel mighty good, when
his eye lighted on a curved dent in the sand.

1

In an instant he had the cap back on his head, snatched up his gun, and was squatting beside the spot, staring at the roundness that could be nothing but a moccasin heel. There was no betraying mark anywhere else, for pine needles blotted out the story of those who had walked here.

Sharply on guard, Rod straightened up and looked around him. The footprints led south along the cross trail. According to his calculations, an area of wild orange grove should lie in that direction. But it was early for the fruit to ripen, and he doubted the Indians had come for that.

Watching both woods and trail, he walked south through the pines. To his satisfaction he found another print within a hundred yards, this one etched deeply in a low, mucky spot. And before he could bend to examine it closely, he saw another and another, rounding the swampy hole and veering northeast.

Lucky he hadn't met these Indians, for the marks were fresh, made within the hour.

Excited at his discovery, he stepped into the shelter of a creeper-laden palm and eyed the woods around him. He'd have to track this band, count them and try to figure out what they were doing here. At Fort Volusia Governor Call was waiting for just such information.

But his personal feelings urged him strongly to hurry on to the fort. The Seminole War was still in its first year, and in 1836 the Florida woods were swarming with hostile braves. Last night, as Rod slept in a palmetto thicket, he had dreamed that a scalping knife cut a neat circle around his crown. The terror of that dream still slashed at him, even though he had fought his fear and crowded it back inside him.

To his right a blue jay squawked. Rod halted, fingers still on his powder horn. Standing still as the trees around him, he listened, pouring all his five senses into one.

Minutes passed. He heard nothing but the gentle brushing of wind in the treetops and fragments of bird song breaking the stillness. A tiny scratching was a squirrel darting up a pine. From the undergrowth came the faint crackle of leaves where a blue-tailed lizard moved.

The squawk of another jay marked the exact spot of the woods' invasion. Then Rod's ears picked up the dim clanking of harness and the creak of wheels.

Nerves tense, he slipped deeper into the vine tangle. He found it hard to believe that a cart from Volusia was on this trail. For within a mile the path narrowed and only deer could thread their way between the close-growing trees.

A few years ago—before the Indian war—Rod might have stepped into the open, eager to hail the driver and tell him he was heading nowhere. But now he remained in hiding, his gun ready for a quick shot.

The creaking grew louder, sounding above the soft, slow thud of hoofs. Suddenly the sharp crack of a whip shattered the quiet and roused a jarring echo in the woods.

The boy was relieved. This driver wasn't trying to hide.

Again he felt the urge to step forward and say hello, but his new caution prevented him.

Eyes on the trail, he watched a team plod into view. Their heads bobbed with each slow step, their harness gleamed in the late shafts of sunlight. The crude cart behind them carried a load covered with dirty canvas.

Rod was glad he had kept still. The man on the wagon seat was a Spaniard, whom he had seen once at Volusia, drunken and singing. He was middling tall, wore a greasy hunting shirt with a bullet hole near the shoulder, and looked stringy-tough as a weathered fence rail. His tangled black hair hung almost to his shoulders, and his eyes were dark as swamp water.

Suspicious, Rod watched the cart bump past. His eyes probed the canvas that concealed the load, but he could not guess what lay under it.

Cautiously, flitting on silent feet from tree to tree, he followed the Spaniard back into the woods. If the man had lost his way he would turn soon. If not, Rod wanted to know the reason.

Ears alert, he listened for Indians, too. The noise of this cart would attract them, he was certain.

The wagon began to slow as the trail narrowed. At last it creaked to a stop. Rod waited, crouching in the midst of a sapling grove. Again came the crack of the whip.

The boy shrank deeper into hiding. The sound must be a signal. Its echo jumped back and died away. Then, warily, an Indian stepped from the woods, moved toward the cart. In a few seconds other Seminoles sifted out from the trees. Five ponies were led to the edge of the trail.

Rod's heart gave a sharp thump. Here were the Indians he had been following! He counted fifteen. Like all Seminoles they wore bright-colored cotton tunics, deerskin moccasins, and gay turbans on their heads. One important-looking warrior carried a rawhide bundle under his arm.

The woods were quiet and voices came clearly to Rod. "We have brought the box," said the brave with the bundle. He spoke in the chuckling guttural of the Seminole tongue, but Rod understood, for he had long ago learned the Indian language.

"Good," grunted the Spaniard.

The Indian's next words jolted Rod. "Have you the gunpowder?"

Even before the war there had been a law against selling gunpowder to the Indians. Any white man who did so was a traitor.

"Show me the silver," the trader demanded, his eager tongue stumbling over the English words.

The Indian unwrapped the bundle slowly. Beneath the rawhide was a lining of soft doeskin. As the inner wrapping slipped away, Rod saw a small silver chest, heavily ornamented. Even at a distance he could tell it was of great value, but of some strange foreign make, with a man's jut-nosed face molded into one side.

The Seminole held it forward, laid it in the teamster's arms.

Rod could sense the Spaniard's greediness as he received the box, but in the manner of a trader he looked it over critically. "It is small," he complained, "not even as big as one of the kegs I give you."

The Indian did not reply. Rod thought he saw a shadowy smile on the brave's lips.

The driver lifted the box lid, looked inside carelessly and closed it again.

Puzzled, Rod wondered if the chest was empty. It seemed strange that the trader would take an empty box. Yet the silver used to make it was worth far more than a few kegs of gunpowder.

"Unload," the Spaniard commanded with a grandiose gesture.

The Indians hurried to obey. Quickly they lowered the tail of the cart and yanked away the dirty canvas, revealing ten kegs of powder in two neat rows. The kegs were rolled gingerly off the wagon and lugged to the ponies. In a few minutes the canvas lay tumbled on the cart bottom and the last keg was being tied onto an Indian mount.

The Spaniard, oblivious, stroked the silver chest, letting his grimed fingers explore its intricate design. At last he set the chest on the seat beside him, reached for the old canvas and covered his treasure carefully. When it was well concealed, he gestured to the Indian leader:

"Semoli—come!"

The Indian moved forward uncertainly.

"If I get guns, how much you give for them?"

"Guns?" repeated the brave, his teeth flashing in a sudden smile. "Much. We give much for guns."

"More silver?"

The warrior turned to an older Indian and the two whispered together.

"We will give hides," the spokesman replied.

The driver flipped his whip. "Hides," he grunted contemptuously.

"There is no more silver," answered the Indian soberly.

"No more? Where have you found this?"

The warrior evaded the question. "We have no more."

"No gold either?"

"We have no gold."

"There is much risk to me in bringing guns," argued the driver. "These I cannot bring unless you pay in silver or gold."

Again the two Indians conferred. The trader watched them sharply.

"I want no hides," he barked as the Seminole stepped forward again.

"We have only hides," said the brave, a note of pleading in his voice. "They are good hides, strong and smooth to the hand. They can be sold for money."

The trader's voice was stone-hard. "I must have silver or gold."

The Indian bowed his head slightly. "We will send among the bands. Perhaps someone has such a thing."

The teamster straightened up, plainly pleased with his bargain. "I will bring the guns in four days."

"Four days," repeated the Indian.

"The sun will stand where it is now," added the trader. "I will crack the whip as I did today."

The Indian nodded. "We will wait for you in the woods."

He hurried to his pony and turned it back into the pines. The rest of the band followed. The rumps of their horses disappeared among the trees and only the team driver was left on the trail.

He wasted no time. With a flick of his whip he set the horses to straining forward. Rod wondered where he was going. But in another minute the team turned sharply into a small clearing, made a circle around a clump of oaks and started back on the trail. The Spaniard burst into a folk song of his homeland, careless who might hear.

This must be an old meeting place, thought Rod. That clearing afforded just enough room to turn. The driver knew it was there and went no farther.

As the team started back, Rod faded quietly into the woods. It was time for him to make tracks for camp. He could keep ahead of the cart, but he must remember to watch for Indians.

Although his blood was racing, he thought clearly. Governor Call, commanding officer of the armies in Florida, must have this information, and quickly. For here was a serious leak of arms—a planned, steady sale of powder and guns to the enemy. It would mean just that many more white men killed in the bloody struggle for the peninsula.

It would be easy to capture the trader when he brought guns the next time. The army would see to that. It was Rod's job to get the news to the army.

With long, swift steps he loped through the forest, following animal trails and returning to the road only when he had left the team far behind. He thought over what he would tell the governor, and rehearsed the scene in the woods so that every detail would remain sharp in his mind.

Still shocked by his discovery, he wondered if this was the only trading of guns and powder—or were such things happening all along the frontier? Most folks were honest, but it took only a few like the Spaniard to build up the enemy's power. Stopping this one flow of weapons might shorten the war by many days.

Rod thought, too, about the chest, with its silver glitter and the weird face. From what far land had it come, and where had the Indians found it? There weren't any silver mines in Florida, and it didn't look like a box the Seminoles might have made themselves. Perhaps they had traded it, long ago, and kept it in the nation as a precious object.

The sun set and darkness crept into the forest, but Rod was nearing Volusia and knew his way. After several hours, the woods thinned, and suddenly he saw the pickets around the encampment. It was peaceful there under the quiet starlight, and the little fort on the St. Johns River did not look like a place for fighting.

He found Governor Call in the south blockhouse, at his desk. Although it was late the man was poring over a book. He looked up as Rod entered, his fine face tortured with doubt of himself, for he had been assailed from all sides as to his conduct of the war.

"Good evening, scout."

Rod saluted. "Good evening, sir. Reporting on a three-day trip below Volusia."

Governor Call laid his book aside and leaned stiffly back in his chair. "Find anything?"

Rod tried not to appear too proud. "Yes, sir. A Spaniard's selling ammunition to the Indians. Today he gave them ten kegs of gunpowder."

The governor's face showed his concern. "Gunpowder!"

"He's going to deliver guns in four days, sir," added Rod, "at the same place."

"Guns, too? Well—good enough. We'll catch him." The man drew a map from a drawer and picked up his pen. "Where was this?"

"About eight miles below the fort, sir, near the wild orange groves."

"Here, would you say?" The pen touched a point on the river.

"A little farther over, sir. There, I think."

Governor Call made a tiny x and drew out a sheet of

plain foolscap. "Now, Rod," he ordered brusquely, "describe this man. Everything you can remember."

"Well, sir, he was a Spaniard . . ."

"Not a half-breed?"

"No, sir, I'm sure of that. He didn't speak Seminole, although he understood it. Besides, he didn't look like an Indian."

"Good. Go ahead."

Rod described the teamster, leaving out nothing, not even the bullet hole in the man's hunting shirt.

"And his cart?" asked the governor.

Rod hadn't been able to observe the cart as carefully as he wanted, but he gave a general description and told about the old canvas covering the load.

"Now, there's one thing I've been wanting to ask you," said the governor, as he dried his writing with a sprinkle of sand. "What did the Indians use for money? They're impoverished. They get some ammunition from Cuba, but they usually pay with hides or furs. Did this fellow take the same?"

Rod shook his head, a faint smile curving his lips. "He took a silver chest, sir."

The governor stared. "A chest? Did you see it closely?"

"Close enough, sir."

"Sure it was silver?"

Rod nodded emphatically. "It was the shiniest thing I ever saw, sir, and molded like a cheap chest wouldn't be." He described the face he had seen.

"Sounds like something from Mexico," noted the executive thoughtfully. "What was inside?"

"I couldn't see that, sir," Rod admitted. "The fellow looked into the box just once, then slapped the top down. So I think, sir, the chest was empty."

"Thinking and knowing are not the same, scout," warned the governor.

"Yes, sir."

"How many Indians were in the band?"

"Fifteen, sir."

"Excellent!" praised the governor. "You've done a fine job of seeing everything, Rod. And you're a good lad to bring it to me so quickly. Now, anything else you want to add?"

Rod thought for a moment. "I believe not, sir."

"Then good night. A good rest to you."

"Thank you, sir."

"And, scout," the man called after him, "keep the whole thing quiet."

"Yes, sir."

Rod walked thoughtfully down the dirt path through the tent area where most of the soldiers lived and slept. It was still a little while before taps, and some of the men were smoking their pipes and talking beside the big fires while others wrote letters by the flickering stub of a candle, or played cards.

Rod spoke to many of them, for the troops had been in camp long enough to get acquainted, but his thoughts were far away, on the battles these men might soon be fighting. From what he had seen, the Indians had no thought of surrendering to be shipped west to Arkansas, as the treaties demanded. They were laying up powder and weapons, readying again for war.

So were the white men. Even now a new general was on his way—Thomas S. Jesup—who would bring mounted troops and hundreds of Creek Indians to engage in a fresh campaign.

It bothered Rod. Not only did he hate war, but he found it hard to fight Indians. He had been in the big battle on the Withlacoochee last spring, been shot at, and seen men die of gun wounds. But he still remembered the friendly bands at Fort Brooke, who let him share the coontie-thickened stews in their sofke kettles.

Most of all, his feelings were mixed up because of the Indian boy Shakochee, whom he had met near the fort on Tampa Bay. The two of them had played ball together, gone on coon hunts and traded woods secrets. Now Shakochee had gone with the warring bands, and many a time the white boy had lowered his gun, hands shaking, as he thought he saw his friend among the painted enemy.

Maybe if he never had known Shakochee, he would like war better, Rod thought to himself.

Inside his tent he found his two friends, John Fox and Hart Whitley, playing cribbage beside a smoky candle. The three had somehow managed to stay together for almost a year of the war, even though Fox was a volunteer infantryman and the two others were scouts.

Hart was the cautious, thoughtful one who influenced Rod most. He hated the war and believed the Indians had been treated unjustly, even though he fought them and had done outstanding service. Fox had criticism for both Indians and whites—his sharp tongue belabored whomever he believed at fault. Hart said some day Fox's talk would land him in jail. But the soldier retorted he hadn't studied law for nothing, and he'd have his say about the Territory and still remain free.

Hart's blue-gray eyes met Rod's as the boy ducked into the tent. The older scout had been worried, Rod knew, for it was getting late and the three-day trip should have ended earlier.

"Just get back?"

"Just now. Been talking to the governor."

John Fox, who had merely said hello, looked up suddenly. "What happened?"

"Nothing I can tell," replied Rod.

Fox's sharp eyebrows rose. "So? Must we smother our curiosity? Come, Roddie, my boy, tell your Uncle John."

"Sorry, sir, I can't," said Rod, faintly embarrassed.

Fox gave an impatient gesture. "Out with it!—It's bad manners to have secrets."

Rod looked at his friend, uncertain whether he was serious or joking. But Fox looked solemn as a treed raccoon. "I can't tell, sir," Rod repeated.

"Don't let him bother you," advised Hart. "He's only a fellow with book learning, and I take it you've got instructions from the governor. This is one time you can tell him to shut up—even if you should respect his age. Had anything to eat?"

Rod relaxed. Now that he had time to think about it, he was terribly hungry. He had eaten some jerked meat at noon and had expected to be home hours earlier.

"I sure need something. Anything left from your supper?"

Fox rummaged in a haversack near by and brought out a thick wedge of fruitcake. "Pork, my boy, and this," he observed. "We saved them both, and I don't mind telling you it was hard to hang onto the cake. Hart, got any biscuits to go with the bacon?"

"Right here."

Hart put the cribbage board aside and began to rustle a supper for Rod. When the boy insisted he could get his own, the older scout brushed him aside. "I feel like a setting hen after three weeks in camp. Let me move around a bit."

In less than half an hour a fire had been built, the bacon fried and coffee boiled. Rod sat down to enjoy his feast.

"What's the news here?" he asked.

Fox looked at Hart. "Might as well tell him now," he said with a shrug. "We leave tomorrow for Wahoo Swamp to fight Indians."

"Wahoo?" repeated Rod in surprise. "But I thought . . ."

"Whatever you thought was wrong," interrupted Fox.

Bewildered, Rod turned to Hart. He had believed he was back in camp—at least long enough for a good night's sleep. Now they were telling him he would go with them to Wahoo Swamp, on the Little Withlacoochee. It was several days' march west into the heart of Indian country.

"I know what you thought," Hart said kindly. "So did we. So did everybody. We were waiting for General Jesup. But now it turns out we aren't waiting at all. Tomorrow morning we march."

Rod tried to hide his dismay. "Looks like quite a battle coming up," he remarked between mouthfuls of fruitcake.

Hart replied slowly, "Wahoo Swamp is the stronghold of the enemy."

Chapter 2

Wahoo Swamp

"The result of the expedition to Wahoo Swamp was a
lesson to other commanders. To force so large a body
of troops, horse and foot, into the enemy's country,
without a base of operations, is a sacrifice of human
life. . . ."

—John T. Sprague
in *The Florida War*

FOUR COLUMNS of soldiers pushed southwest from
Volusia through dense forests matted with creeper,
over sun-baked pine barrens and around black-muck
swamps. The Florida men wore deerskin or homespun,
with tail-trimmed fur caps on their heads. The artillery-
men were in army fatigue uniforms, and the two columns
at the left, some seven hundred Creek Indians, were as
brightly garbed as the Seminole enemy, but turbaned in
white to distinguish them from their foe.

The foot soldiers were followed by more than a thousand mounted fighters from Tennessee who had just come
into the Territory and were expected to turn the war's tide.

At first the men were in high spirits. For months the
army had hunted in vain for a concentration of Indians

17

big enough to give battle. Last spring an entire campaign had failed for lack of an enemy in force. Now, at last, Seminoles had been discovered at Wahoo Swamp. It was said they had built villages there and would defend them.

A victory would even the summer score. For the Indians had attacked Fort Micanopy, arrogantly destroyed the sugar works of General Clinch, and in small bands had raided up and down the Territory.

But as the columns moved slowly along, often chopping their own road and forced to build their own bridges, the men's optimism oozed away.

"Seems like the country's got us beat," remarked one of the Tennesseans, who had wandered up to the evening campfire built by Rod and several others. "We got over a thousand horses back there, and no forage, nothing but this scrub."

"Bring feed for the entire trip?" asked Fox briskly, his sharp eyes searching the man's face.

"Not by a long shot."

Hart had risen from his blanket and offered the man a seat beside the fire.

"No, thanks, got to get back."

"What are you fellows going to do for feed?" persisted Fox.

The man shot him a scornful glance. "Do? What can we do except bury the animals that die?"

He left them and started back toward the Tennesseans' camp.

"A march like this is all right for the Florida men and the Indians," observed John Fox tartly. "We and the Creeks know what to expect. But when the northerners move in, they get bogged down right away. Forage—anybody that knows Florida wouldn't expect to find forage for a thousand horses!"

"What we need's a supply base," put in Hart.

"Sure we do, and we'd have it in a planned campaign. But we're just darting down to Wahoo Swamp for a quick strike. Trying to act like Indians. Only the army can't. The Seminoles are right when they say it moves like a snail."

The next day Rod heard more critical talk. Even the white-turbaned Creeks were disgusted with the many encumbrances and the need to move slowly in columns. And when the rations were doled out in smaller and smaller quantities, the men became hungry and silent.

But on the last morning of the march, spirits lifted again. Word had come that the Indians were indeed at Wahoo Swamp and could be engaged there.

Rod's hopes soared. He scarcely heard the shouted commands, snorts of the horses and creak of the gun carriages as they took the trail. His mind was busy with the hope that this battle might end the war.

The volunteers' good humor increased as the morning sun rose, glancing first through the thin growth of pines, then climbing the sky, which turned a clear, sharp blue. Mockingbirds caroled noisily in the oak hammocks; squirrels and jays scolded as the columns penetrated their woodlands. Once a gray fox leaped softly across the path of the marchers, and the appearance at the woods' edge of a surprised little skunk set the men to laughing.

Rod was striding along, still chuckling at the tiny furred animal, when he glanced down and saw a bright-colored object almost under his moccasin. He side-stepped quickly and with one hand swept up the small oval. To his surprise it was a miniature painting, done in fresh, clear colors.

As he looked at it, he had a distinctly pleasant feeling. This prim girl, whose brown curls lay so neatly arranged on the shoulders of her pink dress, was nobody he knew. Yet she was so far removed from marching and war that she appealed to him like a memory of home.

With his sleeve he wiped a thin dust film from the picture. When it was clean it appeared so dainty that he suddenly became ashamed of his own worn deerskin tunic and dusty moccasins, stained with berry juice and smudged with the charcoal of campfires.

Anyhow, he reflected thankfully, she couldn't see him, or the berry stains, or his untrimmed hair.

Abruptly he realized that someone would be teasing him, and raised his hand to stuff the miniature into his pocket. But John Fox's commanding drawl stopped him short.

"Hand her over, Rod! Let's have a look."

Rod flushed and hesitated, but Fox held out his hand. "Don't be bashful."

Reluctantly Rod gave him the painting. Fox eyed it

closely, uttered a cluck of approval and passed the miniature to Hart. "Had it with you all the way? Got a good-
looking girl and you're holding out on us?"

"Just picked it up," mumbled Rod.

Hart was kinder. "Wonder how that got here?"

He handed the picture back to Rod, who stuffed it hastily
out of sight, trying to act as if it were no more important
than finding a handful of ripe acorns. When he was alone
he could look at it more closely.

The march continued as the sun climbed high and the
day grew warm. Goldenrod daubed the open, sunny spots
with its gay yellow, and the cool twilight of the oak hammocks felt welcome. Rod wondered when the columns
would reach Wahoo Swamp. John Fox, too, was thinking
about their destination.

"Almost there, wouldn't you say?" he remarked to
Hart.

"Just about," the scout replied. He squinted his eyes
and peered ahead between the marching lines. "See that
hammock land? That rings the swamp, I think."

Rod gazed ahead. Yes, that thick growth of oaks and
cabbage palms would be the woods surrounding Wahoo.
And he thought of the bloody victory dance that had
whirled beneath the branches after last winter's murder
of the Indian agent.

"Look!" he cried suddenly, as his eyes picked up a speck
of bright yellow. "Warriors!"

"Right you are," agreed Hart, his calm voice underlaid

with excitement. And as one speck increased to two and
five and then a dozen flecks of brilliant color, he let out a
low whistle. "Hundreds of 'em!"

"In force at last!" crowed Fox. "Now maybe we'll have
something to show for our pains, instead of one captured
old squaw or a couple of papooses."

Orders to halt were coming down the line. The long
columns jerked to a stop. As the creak of the artillery died
away and the sound of many feet marching, a far-off Indian
war cry came to Rod's ears: "Yo-ho-hee! Loo loo yo-ho-hee!"

Now he could see more Seminoles at the edge of the
hammock, their bright shirts and head scarves high-lighted
against the dark woods. As he watched, they came from
between the trees and filtered back into their shadows,
shouting, leaping and crying "Yo-ho-hee!"

"We've caught 'em," remarked Hart quietly. "They're
here, lots of 'em."

The troops were ordered at once into battle formation.
The artillery and Florida volunteers—which included Rod,
Hart and Fox—were strung out in two lines, followed by
a reserve of two companies.

"Forward, march!"

They started toward the hammock, the cannon bumping
over grass clumps and sinking into miry places. Though
frontiersmen and Creeks stepped ahead briskly, their in-
stincts were all against this open attack.

Rod was acutely conscious of his gun where it lay
against his arm, of the position of his powder horn and shot

pouch. These things he must know, for when the shooting started he would have to move quickly, his fingers must not fumble, his powder and shot must not be spilled.

Halfway to the thick tree growth, the order to halt rang out. As he stood there with the midday sun flaming down on him, Rod began to fidget. It was harder to stand still, almost within range of the enemy, than to advance. Far to the rear he heard orders being given the Tennesseans.

"Can't see a single Indian," remarked John Fox.

It was true. The hammock looked empty.

"They're around, just the same," warned Hart. "Every tree's got a warrior behind it. They'll make a stand."

"Maybe they've retreated. Maybe that yelling was all just a bluff."

"Nope. They're just getting ready to fight. Bet you a rattlesnake belt."

"No bets now," flung back Fox. "And cut the talk about snakes. I scared off a cottonmouth back a ways."

An order came echoing down the line. "Check your guns!" And a moment later, "Charge!"

Whips stung the horses' flanks and they strained to set the creaking artillery in motion. Again the cannon lurched ahead. The foot soldiers ran, trying to keep their line intact, their guns at ready.

The dusky hammock loomed closer. No smoke puffs lightened the shadows. No deep groan of rifles sounded beyond the swamp. Rod's eyes searched the moss-ragged treetops and the darkness beneath. Nowhere could he see a flick of color or the gleam of a gun barrel. The silence was worse than the noise of battle. It made his stomach knot like a clenched fist.

The artillery splashed through water that reached to the hubs of the cannon carriage. The horses tugged desperately, their hoofs sinking in the mud. But just as the big guns seemed hopelessly mired, they came up on dry ground again and went charging into the hammock.

Still no rifle shots. Could Hart have been wrong? Had the Indians retreated?

The men jogtrotted beneath the great trees. Deeper and deeper they penetrated the forest. Thinking they had the enemy on the run, they began to shout.

Like a broad wall of sound came the battle cry. "Yo-ho-hee!" Indian colors began to flash through the woods like tropical birds. A rifle volley sounded. Screaming, a horse reared against his traces. Bullets thupped against the tree bark, and a soldier cried out as he fell.

The deep thunder of the first cannon fire smashed against Rod's eardrums. Again—and again. The earth quivered.

He stepped behind the latticed bole of a palm. His body didn't seem a part of him. His hands on the gun felt miles away. But as he sighted along the familiar barrel, the clenched fist inside him relaxed, his grip became firm. Once again the old courage flowed over him as it had that day last winter in his first action.

Directly in his gunsight a yellow shirt inched from

behind an oak. Rod's arm steadied his gun against the bit
of color. His hand squeezed the trigger.

The gun kicked and its shattering sound rang in his
ears. Ahead, the bark of the oak splintered outward. The
Seminole moved back through the woods to new hiding.

A sense of relief possessed Rod. He was glad he had not
killed this stranger.

Careful to stay behind his own sheltering palm trunk,
he reached for shot and powder, jammed the patch-wrapped
ball into his gun barrel, and measured powder into the pan.
Again he peered from behind the tree.

As he searched for sight of the enemy, a ball whizzed
toward him, struck, and jolted him backward. A sharp pain
slit through the flesh above his ribs.

He fell to his knees, crept behind his tree and clung
to its trunk, while one hand felt inside his hunting shirt.
To his amazement his hand encountered the miniature
painting, wet with blood. He pulled it free of his flesh and
the pain stopped. Puzzled, he stared at the oval. Its frame
was twisted and almost severed at the top. The round
imprint of a ball showed plainly.

His fingers sought the wound. It was bleeding, but not
hard. The ribs seemed unhurt.

He shoved the picture back inside his shirt and again
primed his gun. Suddenly angry, he fought more furiously
than before, pursuing Indians from tree to tree and shooting with deadly accuracy. This time he wanted to kill. He
wounded one brave, saw him dragged to safety by his fel-

lows. Another disappeared, and Rod could see no body, living or dead.

Slowly he moved ahead. Sometimes he was aware that men in the line were falling. He could not pause to help them. He must push the enemy back.

Gradually the woods emptied. It was hard to find a target. The troops moved faster. At last the forest thinned and a wide swamp lay before them.

"Halt!"

The dismal area of mud and water stretched for half a mile. Wide-boled cypress trees rose from it, and in places it was thick with sawgrass or flat green lily pads.

Orders came to skirt the swamp, but there was no high land anywhere. Moccasins sank ankle-deep into the black ooze, and the heavy cannon had to be half lifted through the morass. When the water deepened, the cannon began a wider detour. Foot soldiers held their guns and powder high as the black earth yielded and the water rose nearly to their waists.

Above them buzzards planed through the bright blue sky, or sat humped on a bare branch of cypress. Now and then Rod saw a snake rippling the water's surface, and his skin prickled as he glimpsed a deadly moccasin.

Nobody talked. The men had fought hard, hoping to win. But once again the foe had vanished, almost into thin air, and the soldiers still were pursuing, bone-tired, some of them wounded, through endless reaches of swamp and hammock.

From the left came rifle fire and war whoops, where the Creeks had caught up with some of the Seminoles. And far to the right sounded a volley from the Tennesseans.

At last the earth firmed, the foot soldiers left the swamp. And on the banks of the Little Withlacoochee they again saw Indians.

The men fought with desperation now, firing volley after volley at the tree-protected enemy. A rain of lead came from across the river. Near Rod a man fell, a spreading red stain on his shirt. Another, dragging a leg, staggered back toward the swamp.

Were these bullets sent by the gunpowder in the Spaniard's kegs? Rod wondered. Had it found its way here into this black death hole, where no side could grasp victory?

The gunfire thinned, stopped. The phantoms had again vanished. The men waited, not talking, wondering if this was all of the battle. Had they won or lost? There seemed to be no answer.

Toward evening came the order to retreat.

Back at camp that night, three miles from the swamp, the fires had never seemed so welcome. The men talked of the day's action and ate their scanty rations, grumbling because there was no pork with their hard bread and only weak coffee. It was just talk, a way to cover their relief at still being alive.

Nobody felt victorious. Although they had pushed back the enemy, their fatigue had soaked into them, as the swamp waters had been absorbed by their clothes.

The volunteers refilled their powder horns and their shot pouches. Wet moccasins were hung in front of the flames and muddy guns were cleaned.

John Fox sat between Hart and Rod, busily polishing his rifle barrel.

"Hart was right," he said thoughtfully. "This is too far to bring an army big as this one without a supply base. You can't ram thousands of men through the wilderness. You can't tote enough to feed 'em, and of course the horses can't find enough forage."

Rod spoke up: "If we have to chase Indians, we have to go where they are."

"Then we ought to travel the way they do," replied Fox curtly.

Rod agreed. He turned his moccasins bottom side toward the fire and tossed another stick of pitch pine onto the flames. Idly he noted two notches on the walnut butt of Fox's gun.

"What are those for—Indians?" he asked, thinking Fox had killed two of the enemy.

"Nope," replied Fox shortly. "Those are broken promises."

"Broken promises?"

"Yep."

Rod was curious. "Whose?"

"Ours."

Rod was flabbergasted. "Tell me what you mean, John," he urged. "I don't understand."

"Well, this is the Treaty of Fort Moultrie," said Fox, pointing to the top notch. "We promised the Indians twenty years in Florida and then we didn't give it to them. Too many white people wanted Florida land."

Rod's face was serious. "That isn't funny."

"No, it certainly isn't funny," Fox rejoined, his eyes cold. "But truth is truth, and the Treaty of Fort Moultrie is all written out in black and white in the official records. Go look, if you don't believe me."

"I believe you," assured Rod. "I know it's true. Still, I don't think you ought to put it so bluntly."

"It won't make me popular," agreed Fox, arching an eyebrow. "But too much discretion makes for dishonesty. The treaty said twenty years. That's what the Indians remember. That's what we forgot."

"I think, too, we should have held to the terms of the treaty," Rod admitted. "But what about the Indians not turning in runaway slaves?"

"That I haven't considered worth a notch," explained John Fox, rubbing vigorously at the smooth wood. "Proof is lacking that they failed in their part of the bargain."

Rod couldn't deny that. "What's the second notch?"

"Well, it isn't the treaty of Payne's Landing or the Treaty of Fort Gibson, as you might expect," Fox replied, his eyes sharp as bayonets. "Those two treaties didn't represent the Indians, to my mind. Micanopy didn't sign at Payne's Landing, neither did King Philip, Osceola, or lots of others. The tribes just weren't represented. And why should they sign up to go to Arkansas, a country they never had seen?"

The truth of his talk made Rod uneasy. "A few chiefs went," he answered. "They signed the Treaty of Fort Gibson."

"Seven chiefs!" exploded Fox. "Seven only! And they didn't have authority to sign such a treaty, according to the Indians. They were to find out if Arkansas land was good. Wasn't that right?"

"That's the way I understand it."

"They didn't like it. They said their old enemies, the Creeks, lived there. Then they turned around and signed the treaty! Would you be mad if you were a Florida Indian and that happened to you?"

Rod changed the subject. "Then what *is* the other notch?"

Fox laughed shortly. "The agreement with General Gaines. He promised the Indians could stay south of the Withlacoochee and would be let alone until commissioners were sent to make a treaty."

"I don't go along with that, John," Rod objected. "Neither side was empowered to make a treaty that time, and both said so."

"True. But a United States general did make a promise and another general, Scott, went right ahead and carried out his campaign without paying any attention to the palaver."

"Still I can't go along with that. Why haven't you any notches for the Indians?"

"Oh, I have." To Rod's surprise, Fox turned the gun over and revealed a notch on the other side. It was tiny, a mere sliver out of the walnut.

"It's pretty small."

"That's because it's for one man, Osceola, the time he was in jail at Fort King. He said he would abide by the two treaties. Of course he said it to get out of jail. But it was a lie."

Rod did not answer. What could one reply? He could find nothing untrue in what Fox had said, but the man's sarcasms worried him. The United States allowed freedom of speech, yet it did not seem loyal for a soldier, even a short-term volunteer, to say such things.

He gazed across the campfires and into the black depths of the pines, trying to figure out what was right. And suddenly he knew that truth itself was a higher ideal than loyalty without truth. And it became clear to him that Americans must speak out their disapproval of whatever wrong they had done as a body, so that things could be corrected.

He saw, too, that nothing here could be changed and brought back to the beginning. Mistakes had tangled things hopelessly. Now there was only the situation as it existed. There was no going back, only the hope that things would be right in the future.

He was roused from his thoughts by Hart, who laid a hand on his shoulder.

"Better get to bed. We start early in the morning for Volusia. They've caught your Spaniard."

Rod stiffened. "Who is he?"

"His name is Zade Galda. He's hauled a lot of stuff for the army."

"Galda," repeated Rod.

"They want you to identify him and tell what you saw."

"Yes, sir."

"Go to bed. I'll see about getting horses for the two of us."

Chapter 3

Capitulation

"I have seen the court sit in a store where barrels of
pork and flour formed seats for thc audience."
—Achille Murat
in *America and the Americans*

JUDGE PARTON leaned forward in his log chair,
the only chair in the small cabin, and looked quizzi-
cally at the boy standing before him.

"Ever testified, son?"

"No, sir," replied Rod.

"Nothing hard about it," the judge assured him. "Just
telling the truth is all you have to do."

"Yes, sir."

Rod was grateful for the words. The angry-eyed Spaniard at one side of the room and the silent knot of army
officers at the other bothered him, made his throat tighten
as he laid his hand across the judge's shabby Bible.

He repeated the oath slowly: "I hereby swear to tell the
truth, the whole truth and nothing but the truth, so help
me God."

The judge laid the book aside. "Now tell me"—the wise

33

eyes looked deep into Rod's—"did you ever see this man before?"

Rod glanced quickly at the prisoner. "Yes."

"He lies!" burst out the teamster. "I have not seen him before, this boy!" He was silenced by the prick of a bayonet.

"Where, Rod?" asked the judge.

"Eight miles south of Volusia," Rod continued.

"What was he doing?"

"He brought ten kegs of powder to the Indians. They gave him a silver chest."

The prisoner's eyes met Rod's. In their black depths there was so much enmity that Rod's hand slid toward his belt knife. The judge reached out and drew the arm back.

"Don't worry, lad. The law will take care of him right proper. Now go ahead. What was the silver chest like?"

Rod looked back at the judge, and under the man's kindly gaze he described the chest, not forgetting the strange face on one side of it. He finished by saying, "This fellow told the Indians he would come back in four days with guns for them. Then he rode off in his cart."

Some of the officers began whispering and the judge called for silence. He leaned forward, looking intently at Rod. "You're sure it's the same man?"

Rod felt no doubt. "Yes, your honor. He's the one. I even told Governor Call about the bullet hole in his hunting shirt."

"Hmm." The judge eyed the small round hole in the

Spaniard's jacket, near the collarbone. He glanced sharply at the prisoner as if to say, "There's a story there, but it can wait for another time."

"On what date did you see this man, Rod?"

"November twentieth, sir, the day before we started our march to Wahoo Swamp."

"What time of day?"

"Middle of the afternoon, sir."

Judge Parton leaned back, cogitated. "Have you ever heard of a man named Zade Galda?"

"Somebody told me that was his name, sir. I didn't know it before."

"Wasn't any name mentioned that day in the woods?"

"No, sir."

"Thank you, Rod. That's enough, I guess. You may go. Bring the prisoner forward."

Rod went outside to where Hart was waiting.

"How was it?" asked the scout.

"All right, I guess," replied Rod. His voice sounded funny—hoarse and different. He had just sent a man to jail and he didn't like the feeling it gave him. "What do you think he'll get?"

"Don't know," the scout said carelessly. "Enough, I hope."

"Maybe it won't be too long."

"Too long!" exclaimed Hart. "What d'you mean?"

The astonishment in his friend's voice made Rod wish he'd kept still. "Nothing, I guess."

Almost roughly Hart seized Rod by one shoulder and twirled him around so they faced each other. Hart's eyes were incredulous. "What do you mean 'too long'?"

Rod stared, taken aback by the scout's sudden anger. For a moment he couldn't speak.

Hart kept talking. "He's not just a fellow who made a mistake and broke a law. He's a murderer!"

"Murderer?" faltered Rod.

"Sure!" raged Hart. "That ammunition'll kill some of us fellows in the next battle. Maybe you, maybe me, maybe Fox or our other friends!"

Rod nodded, his face pale. "You're right."

"Then what are you crying about?"

"I'm not crying."

"Not now, maybe, but you were. Shedding a sentimental tear for a fellow that had to go to jail because he committed a crime. What ails you?"

"I don't know," mumbled Rod, ashamed. "I don't feel that way now."

"There's a time to be soft and a time to be hard," Hart scolded. "Better get straight on it."

"I will."

Hart was cooling off. "I'm sorry. I didn't mean to fly off the handle."

"That's all right."

Rod swung into step beside his tall friend as the two of them turned toward camp. He had been bawled out, but he felt better.

"Just one more thing," said the scout, as he waggled a warning finger at Rod, "Galda won't feel sorry for you—ever. He'll be after you the minute he's free. Remember that."

The few short, nippy spells of winter slowly gave way to the warmth of early March. New patches of green flowed out from the oaks, and white dogwood blossoms drifted through the forest. Flocks of robins, bound for the north, flashed their orange breasts across the sky, or sometimes lighted in a rosy horde on a broad-branched tree.

At Fort Dade, built on the spot where Major Dade's two companies had been massacred little more than a year before, there was much excitement. The Indians were coming in.

Through the Indian chief, Alligator, General Jesup had arranged a meeting on March sixth.

For a while nobody had expected the Seminoles to attend another conference, especially since General Jesup had made it clear that the United States ordered them to leave Florida. Some two hundred of them had attacked Fort Mellon in February, and during the first three months of the year, the white armies had hunted them down relentlessly—when they could find them.

But as Jumper, Davy and Cloud drifted in with their followers, optimism grew. Perhaps something could be settled at last between white and red.

Rod and Hart had been sent to the fort as interpreters.

Both knew the Seminole language and would be useful at the talks.

Although Rod still carried the girl's picture in his pocket, he had shown it to no one since that first day. He had straightened the frame a little, but it still was badly bent and would always bear the imprint of the ball. Sometimes he got out the painting when he was alone and thought no one would see. And one of those times he discovered something he had overlooked before—tiny writing across the back:

Dolly James
St. Augustine

He vowed that if he ever got to that city, he would look her up. Even if she turned out to be rich, and not interested in farm boys, he wanted to return the picture and tell her what had happened. John Fox said the ball couldn't have been fired with a proper charge of powder, and pointed out that the Indians were careless in loading their guns, so that sometimes a bullet struck without injuring. But Rod felt sure the trinket had saved him from a severe wound.

Outside the tent he heard the light tread of Hart's moccasins and stuffed the miniature back into his pocket.

"Two more chiefs have come in!" Hart announced jubilantly as he stuck his head between the tent flaps, "and the palaver's beginning. Come on!"

Rod scrambled to his feet. The more chiefs, the better

conference. The better conference, the more chance of peace in Florida.

"Here's hoping!" he exclaimed earnestly as he strode beside Hart toward the blockhouse.

"I pray it'll come to something good."

At the log fort, they found General Jesup seated stiffly in a pinewood chair, the Indians ranged in a semicircle before him. The middle-aged general gazed with uncompromising sternness at the Indians. He had been a military man all his life and now took the view that treaties had been made and must be kept. Various army officers were seated beside him, while the chiefs were backed by their followers, including two Negro interpreters.

The stern-faced general motioned Hart and Rod to stand close behind him. "We've been waiting for you," he said when the two took their places. "I want you to translate as literally as possible. If there's any disagreement between you about the meaning of one thing or another, let me know. I want no misunderstandings in this document."

"Yes, sir," replied the two scouts, saluting.

The room was still while they waited for the white chief to begin. Rod's temples throbbed as he glanced at the Indians, whose decision would mean so much to the territory. In contrast to their bright clothing and the colorful bird feathers in their hair, their faces were closed and forbidding.

Jumper, a young Seminole with intelligent eyes and

lithe body, stood at the left. Next to him was Cloud, sometimes known as Yaholoochee, a celebrated warrior who was said to hate the white man. He represented Micanopy. Cloud's face was gloomy. Holatoochee also wore a dark look, as did Horthleematee and John Cawyya.

"First of all," said General Jesup slowly, his firm voice carrying well through the clear air, "I want it plain that we are not here to make a new treaty. Treaties already have been made, signed by the Indian chiefs, and ratified by the United States Congress."

He paused while the Negroes translated to the chiefs, who nodded.

"This conference," continued the general, "is to clarify those treaties and to obtain further signatures from the Indians."

Again the Negroes translated.

"Jumper, what have you to say?" asked the general, fixing his gaze on Micanopy's sense bearer.

Jumper's words were terse and to the point, spoken in Seminole for clearer meaning.

"He says," Hart translated, "that the Indians wish to take their Negro slaves. They have discussed the migration and are willing to move their families at once, but the slaves must go with them."

General Jesup drew out his copies of the last two treaties. Rod could not tell if he was pleased or displeased. His voice came slowly, each word ponderous and full of meaning.

"It is now more than a year past the time the Indians agreed to move west. At Payne's Landing, where a treaty was made, the chiefs agreed to go to Arkansas if the land was suitable. The Great White Father at Washington then sent a delegation of chiefs, who signed another agreement saying the tribes would move."

His voice suddenly grew loud and stern: "Why have not the Indians kept the treaties?"

The Indian chiefs were silent, although their glances were hostile as they listened to the translation by one of the old Negroes. This time they exchanged a few words. Cloud made reply, with Hart again translating.

"The chiefs say they must take their Negro slaves to Arkansas. If they can take the slaves, their warriors will come in, the womenfolk and the children. All will go to the ships."

Thus the conference seesawed back and forth, the Indians sticking to their statement that they must take their Negroes, General Jesup pointing to the violated articles in the treaties. Sometimes the Indians observed that certain provisions had not been kept by the white man, but mostly they seemed discouraged with such arguments. They had presented them long ago, and no one paid much attention.

Jumper made one halfhearted attempt to prove that the last two treaties were not those of the entire nation. But mainly the chiefs returned to the one point: They must be allowed to take their slaves.

In late afternoon, after many words and much repetition, the conference ended, to be resumed next day.

"Why are they so set on taking their slaves?" Rod asked Hart.

"Negroes are part of their life," Hart replied wearily. "The two races have intermarried. Even Osceola's wife was part Negro—the girl Chechoter, who was forced into slavery."

"Yes, I remember," said Rod, recalling his father's anger when Chechoter had been captured.

"The Negroes plead with the Indians not to let them go. Many of them really belong to the Seminoles—others do not want to return to the stricter kind of slavery we have. They're a strong influence."

"Yes," agreed Rod. "But why did some of the chiefs sign those other treaties if they didn't mean to keep them?"

"The chiefs who signed probably meant to keep the treaties," Hart explained. "But they didn't represent the nation, as the Indians said today. It isn't just an argument—it's true."

The talk made Rod deeply uneasy. "Don't any of the Indians want to go west?" he puzzled. "It seems to me it would be better than fighting."

"Some want to go. Almost three hundred have taken their bands to Arkansas. They say Micanopy himself wants to leave. He's old and fat and hasn't any heart for war."

"Maybe they'll really sail this time."

The next day was no more fruitful than the first until

at last General Jesup, who at first had seemed stone hard, suddenly agreed to let the Indians keep their Negroes.

There was a shifting and a buzz of excited conversation. Even the Indians who did not speak a word of English seemed to know what had been said before the interpreters told them. The gloom vanished. Their answers were quick and emphatic.

"We will go and take our slaves with us."

General Jesup turned to his orderly and asked for the articles of capitulation, which had been revised the night before with this new clause inserted. They were read aloud by the general and translated one by one.

Article V stood out among the rest and would always remain in Rod's mind:

"Major General Jesup, in behalf of the United States, agrees that the Seminoles and their allies, who come in and emigrate to the west, shall be secure in their lives and property; that their Negroes, their bona fide property, shall accompany them to the west; and that their cattle and ponies shall be paid for by the United States at a fair valuation."

It was agreed that the Indians would assemble by April tenth at Fort Brooke on Tampa Bay, there to go aboard ships for the west.

The chiefs departed hurriedly when the conference was over, and General Jesup was congratulated by his officers. The soldiers were exultant. Surely the war was ended. Even Hart said he would go back to Tallahassee and start work again on his small plantation. Much of it had been burned, and the fields had gone to weeds, but he was ready to start clearing for a new crop.

"And you, Rod, are you going home?" he asked as the two of them stood outside the fort.

"My term's up next week. I want to go. I haven't seen my folks for a long time."

"Look," exclaimed the scout, "why don't you go back to the general and ask to be released? I'll stand by for any interpreting he needs."

Rod didn't require urging. He hurried inside the log building, found General Jesup at his desk and asked to be relieved of duty.

The general clapped him on the shoulder heartily. "Go, lad, and welcome. We'll be discharging other troops soon, and you might as well leave at once. It won't be long till the whole Territory can go back home."

"Thank you, sir."

The general turned to his aide. "See that Rod is mustered out today."

Rod raced back to the tent and with hurried, clumsy fingers began tying up his belongings for the trip to Tampa.

Only once did he feel a twinge of doubt. "You think for sure the war's over?" he asked the older scout.

"The Indians are at the end of their rope," replied Hart. "They haven't any food, money or clothes. Their cattle have been shot and their villages burned. So I guess for sure this is the end."

"I hope you're right."

But as he packed, Rod couldn't help but remember the notches on John Fox's gun. Would the Indians keep this treaty? Or would there be another notch under that small one?

Chapter 4

Vengeance

"Transports will be ready to take the Indians and their
Negroes off to their western homes."
—Article IX of the
Fort Dade Capitulation

BACK AT Tampa, Rod joined his family at the cabin
on the bay. The peaceful home that had housed
Uncle Ace and Aunt Cele before the Seminole War now
was protected by a high picket fence of logs fitted with
loopholes for muskets. Ma had planted her vegetable garden outside the shelter, but otherwise the family kept
mostly within the "forted up" home.

It wasn't like being on the old Hillsborough farm. Here
the daily jobs were different. He went shrimping with his
father, or to catch trout and red snapper which they sold
at the fort. But mostly he cared for the nets, hoed the
garden, or brought a bagful of fresh game from the woods.

Once or twice during the spring months he traveled
with his father to the farm. They cut down weeds that
grew rankly around the log dwelling and aired the single
large room.

It was like having a knife twisted in him to see the familiar home deserted. Shorn of all its movement, it was drifting back to become part of the forest. Spanish moss had collected on the fruit trees, the milkshed was full of scampering wood mice, and its roof piled deep with pine needles.

Inside the house the walls were streaked with mould. Even the fire wouldn't draw properly, and from a chimney cranny Rod rescued a swift's nest filled with four white eggs.

As Rod and his father ate their lunch, the boy spoke with hesitant eagerness. "It isn't too late to put in a crop. We could start plowing and plant right away."

Mr. Wheeler shook his head. "When the Indians have gone west, I'll start work on the farm."

It was what he always said.

Sometimes Rod grew too restless for his jobs around Tampa Bay. Then he put a bag on his shoulders and strode into the woods to collect herbs for his mother. She had begun to sell her home remedies—tall brown bottles of bitters, or a liquid made from milkweed root to cure chest ailments. Sometimes when Rod had made a lucky trip, she included the Indian pais-haw, famous as an antidote for rattlesnake bites.

Three weeks after the Fort Dade agreement, General Jesup announced officially that the Seminole War was over. The War Department had approved his promise to the Indians, and everything seemed moving toward a peaceful emigration. But skeptics pointed out that the most warlike among the Indians—Osceola and Coacoochee—had not been present when the document was signed.

The general rejoicing among Florida settlers increased as the Indians began to come in. Back in the forest, ten miles from the fort on Tampa Bay, they established a camp, as they had agreed at Fort Dade.

They put their new blankets, issued by the army, inside the temporary brush shelters they had made, and settled down to wait for the boats that would take them west. Once again the sofke kettles were full above the spoke-wheel fires, a padding of flesh came to cover the ribs of the papooses, and their cheeks rounded out like the fat, rosy peaches of August.

On the army's list of those surrendering were the names of Alligator, Holatoochee, Jumper, Cloud, Micanopy and their followers. Relatives were on the way, the chiefs said.

In line with his declaration that the war was over, General Jesup discharged the militia and volunteers, sent the marines north and ordered regular troops to posts that were free of fevers.

Everywhere people began returning to their homes. Boarded cabins were reopened and new crops entrusted to the warm soil. Even Rod's father seemed to waver in his resolution to wait until the Indians were gone.

Coacoochee visited the fort, talked with the other Indians, and said he would come in soon. Twenty-six schooners sailed into the bay and anchored, ready for the émigrés.

As if to write the final flourish to the emigration story, word came from Fort Mellon that Osceola had surrendered there, been given food and ponies, and was bringing his family to Tampa Bay.

Only one thing smudged the picture of peace: the complaint of Florida and Georgia slaveholders that General Jesup had given their slaves to the Indians. Soon there came a directive from Secretary of War Poinsett in Washington: Let slaves belonging to the white men be given back to them.

Dutifully obeying the command of his military superior, General Jesup told the chiefs they would have to give up all Negroes taken during the war.

With astonishment the Indians received General Jesup's order. A council was called and the chiefs agreed that the Fort Dade treaty was being changed. They need no longer be bound by their promises.

Although slave-catchers came in increasing numbers to the camp, the Indians remained. They watched some ninety slaves removed. They protested angrily, but the white general only repeated what he had said before.

During the warm spring days, while he waited for his father's decision to go home, Rod built himself a rowboat. It was a small, stumpy craft, made of cypress and fitted with a center seat. He cut two stout oars for it and often rowed around the bay when the water was calm. He named it *The Pelican*.

On the afternoon of June second he had rowed up a twisting bayou, drawn the boat into a jumble of mangrove roots until it was completely hidden, and gone on to trade his carved-wood charms with the Seminoles.

To his surprise an air of quiet and secrecy hung over the camp. The new blankets were still inside the brush shelters. The sofke kettles bubbled and the papooses were playing with little wooden guns. But Rod did not find the easy hospitality and quick laughter that had marked his last visit.

The Seminoles seemed uninterested in his lucky pieces, and some merely shook their heads at sight of them. There were no Negroes in sight.

After half an hour of trading, Rod had several things of little value—a bear tail, a broken pistol, and a conch shell said to tell stories if he held it close to his ear.

He asked several times if anyone had seen Shakochee, but no one was acquainted with his friend. Finally Rod found an old man who recognized the name.

"The boy is with Coacoochee," he said. "He will come soon—perhaps."

"Has he been to this camp?"

The old man refused to say more, and Rod did not press him. It was enough to know that his friend was with the fiery Coacoochee, for that warrior had promised to bring in his band.

On his way back to the boat, Rod angled off into the woods, thinking he had better shoot some game before returning home. He had seen three deer on his way to the camp, but his rifle trigger had stuck, and they had bounded off before he could shoot.

He checked powder in the pan, held the weapon at ready, and moved slowly between the trees, possessed by a hunch that game was close by.

Sure enough. He had not walked half a mile before he heard the chuckling gobble of a wild turkey. He walked slowly toward the sound, setting his moccasins softly on the pine needles.

At last he stopped, his eyes searching the trees. The bird call came again, from high in a sycamore. Carefully Rod raised his rifle, caught the cock's red wattles in his sight, and fired.

With a loud squawk, the turkey took flight, but after a few wingbeats dropped heavily through the trees and hit the ground not far from Rod.

With a blow of his knife, the boy finished off the bird and threw it across his shoulder. He was thinking so pleasantly of how the fowl would taste, spitted over the coals, that he did not hear the faint crunch of pine needles behind him. But at the sharp crack of a cone he whirled suddenly.

It was too late. Before he could move to defend himself, a rifle butt whirled toward him, struck the side of his head. There was an instant of pain while his thoughts pivoted dizzily, then deep blackness.

When he came to, Rod was lying on the ground. His head ached throbbingly. He tried to move his hands, but they were lashed behind him. His ankles, too, were tied together.

Near by he heard someone breaking twigs for a fire, and his eyes turned to the spot.

Yes, it was the face he had glimpsed just before the blow—Zade Galda's. The man still wore the hunting shirt with the bullet hole. He was humming a little tune while he fed kindling to the flames. Next him lay a whittled stick, spitted with a breast of turkey.

Zade glanced up. The gleam in his black eyes sharpened. "Buenos dios, muchacho," he said politely. "We meet again. How do you enjoy the vines which tie you?"

Rod did not reply.

"Truly uncomfortable, I am sure," said Galda. "I, too, have felt the hurt of wrists and ankles. I know how you feel."

He had urged the fire to a leaping flame, and now he held the turkey over it, watching with relish the quick browning of the meat and the juice that dripped along the stick.

"It is food for a king," he remarked to Rod. "So good I do not even miss the sauce."

Rod's thoughts were thick and slow to gather. "How'd you get out of jail?" he asked warily.

Galda laughed, his teeth gleaming in the firelight. "That is my secret. Perhaps I shall use the same trick again. I would not tell it."

Rod looked at the man, wondering what he could do to free himself. The ache in his head hampered him. He could think of nothing but Hart's words about Galda: "He'll be after you the minute he's free. Remember that."

"It was a strong jail," bragged the Spaniard, "but they have found it not strong enough for Galda. Only this time," he raised a warning finger, "I will see that no tattling nino sets the soldiers after me."

He paused to turn the fowl, then added slowly: "Why do you wish to know how I have left the jail? Is it your idea to go back and tell again?"

Rod looked at him but did not reply. He could not think what to say to the man, or what to do.

"Curiosity!" snorted the trader. "It has killed a cat, you English say." And, as if the boy had spoken, "Be quiet! You will not learn how I escaped. Nor will you know what I plan for you."

For a few moments there was silence. Galda shifted his hands on the roasting stick.

At last he said, half to himself, "I am a trader. I do not like to throw away. Whatever I have, I trade. Long time ago I have learn that small, no-good things sometimes are worth money. Somebody wants almost anything, no matter how old or broken. So I like not to throw away. I like not to kill either." He paused for a moment, adding coldly, "It might waste."

A shiver ran through Rod. Revolting as Galda's philosophy might be when applied to human life, it was good luck now. He was going to be spared just because Galda was stingy.

"How could you trade me?" he asked, surprise overcoming his caution. "Nobody would buy a white man."

"No," agreed Zade, scratching his head in perplexity. "But I will keep your gun and sell my own—it is not as good. That brings me money. You—I don't know. I have to think. Some way I use you."

Rod was silent. Let the man think he could turn him into money. It didn't matter. The important thing was to live. Maybe he could escape. Perhaps tonight, when Zade was sleeping, he could slip his bonds.

Evening had brought dusk to the forest when the Spaniard finished roasting his turkey. He ate the meat slowly, chewing it with relish, but did not offer any to Rod. Once he caught the boy looking at him, but he glanced away and did not give food to his prisoner.

When the meat was gone, Zade wiped his hands on his hunting shirt, drew out his knife, and burst into a bar of song while he slashed a length of grapevine. He tied the vine around the turkey's feet, tossed a long tendril over a tree limb, and drew the fowl's carcass high, where animals could not reach it.

Another example of the man's thrift, thought Rod. And it proved he meant to stay here, at least for another meal.

Before going, the Spaniard cut a piece of homespun from Rod's shirt and stuffed it roughly between the boy's lips, tying it at the back of his head. Then he picked up the two rifles. With one foot he scattered the fire.

Rod hardly could believe his eyes. The man was going to leave him. He hid his excitement. While he felt sure that Galda would return, he was positive he could escape somehow while the trader was gone.

"Stay quiet," Zade cautioned. "Stay quiet until I come back."

Rod could not answer because of the gag. He lay without moving.

"Dead, you would be worth nothing."

The trader turned and marched off into the woods. Rod waited, listening until the man's footsteps had died away in the distance. He felt better now, and the night air had eased the ache in his head. Hopefully he tried to move his wrists backward and forward. But the vine was tight, too tight for him even to rub one arm against the other.

He tried the ankle vine. It gave a little, but not enough to free him.

Again he strove to loosen the vine around the wrist, but it would not give. He began to sweat, thinking that perhaps his fine chance to free himself would be wasted after all.

Tensing his body, he tested his full strength against the bonds, but they only bit into his bare flesh. He rolled toward a tree and rubbed against it, but the vine held. Nor did a humpy palmetto root fray the hard fiber.

For hours Rod tried to break loose, without luck. His wrists were swollen and bleeding, but tied as firmly as before. Angry now and despairing, he strained hard against the vine, ignoring the pain as it cut into his flesh. But he knew in the back of his mind that the stalk would not give, for it was one of the toughest things in the forest.

Panic rose in him, the panic of frustration, and for a moment he struggled wildly. Gradually his foolish rage subsided, and he lay still, tears leaking out from under his eyelids. Then he struggled again, and again was defeated.

Suddenly his eyes caught the glimmer of a few bright stars through a hole in the forest canopy. Their faraway gleam touched him, as it always did, with a sense of the immensity of space, and a certainty that his own affairs were only as specks of dust in the onward sweep of the universe. One life, perhaps, was not too important, even if it was your own. But bravery must be a great thing, passed on from one life to another, until it bulked large beneath those sky lanterns.

He drew a deep breath. From now on he would be brave.

Chapter 5

Free

"The arrival of several Floridians in camp for the purpose of looking after and apprehending the Negroes spreads general consternation among them. Those Negroes that were in camp fled and carried panic with them, and we cannot now induce them to return."
—Major General Thomas S. Jesup
in a report to Washington

ZADE HAD been gone a long time. Rod may have dozed, he didn't know. Gradually he became aware, as if he had dreamed it, of a gentle sound in the woods. It grew, came closer, and brushed past not a hundred feet away. It was like many footsteps mingled with dim hoofbeats, faint creakings, and the occasional small clank of metal.

It was not a little sound but a vast, quiet one. Startled, Rod listened, expecting it to go away, but it went on and on, like an army marching.

It couldn't be an army, Rod knew. No army ever advanced so softly. When the army marched there was lots of noise—boots thumping, a jingle of spurs, and crisp orders ringing out. Even the volunteers in their moccasins did not march like this.

He raised his head cautiously. Beneath the flicker of torches moved a shadowy caravan of half-naked men. Occasionally a long-tailed pony passed by, carrying a humpy load, and once he saw sleeping children lashed to a slow-moving animal.

Indians—hundreds of them. And they weren't going toward the encampment. They were moving southeast.

At first he thought they might have been sent to bring in other bands. But the presence of children, and the women—he now saw them, too—made that unlikely. His thoughts jumped back to the encampment. There were hundreds of Indians there. Could it be they—going away from camp?

Horror seeped through him. Those hundreds, waiting to be sent to Arkansas, were slipping back into the forests. They had rejected the treaty and were running away.

A liquid whippoorwill call came from where the column moved, then another and another until the cry had echoed all down the line. Yes, the whole caravan was Indians. No one else could mimic so perfectly. They must have left camp without being seen. Now they were well on their way to new hiding spots.

Beneath Rod's strong sense of disaster at this violation of the Dade agreement was a grudging realization that the Dade promises were based on old, unfair treaties.

The Indians were taking their turn at being unfair. They had received blankets and money for their cattle; they had eaten well for months. Again they were ready to fight.

He was glad they hadn't come closer to where he lay. For the war was on once more, and he would be counted an enemy.

The caravan had almost passed when a brave suddenly cried out. Hastily he snatched a torch from another warrior and turned in Rod's direction. Others followed. A chilly sweat enveloped the boy. Could they have seen him? It seemed unlikely. Then, as the brave pointed, Rod knew what had caught his eye—the half-plucked turkey carcass gleaming in the torchlight.

Near the fowl the first warrior stopped abruptly, raised his flaming stick. "Wait!" he cried in Seminole. A second Indian half raised his rifle. The others crowded close behind. The swaying light of the torch contorted their faces.

"See!" shouted one of them suddenly, pointing at Rod.

The man with the gun raised it sharply and took aim, but the torch carrier pushed him aside. "He is tied."

Cautiously they came closer. Above his terror, Rod was thinking coolly, searching their faces for one he knew. They were all strange. He tried to call out, "I am Luckmaker!" but the words were lost in the folds of his gag.

The warriors came close and stood around him. Gun muzzles gaped at him. He tried again to speak, but the words were lost.

A brave approached, gripping a knife. Rod cringed as

the blade moved toward his throat. But the fellow only slit his gag and lifted it away.

"I'm Luckmaker!" Rod cried at once through stiff lips. "Don't you know me?"

No one answered.

"I carve lucky pieces. Don't you remember?"

More silence. Finally someone said in Seminole, "He is not lucky now."

No one laughed at the grim joke.

"Let us take him," a steady voice commanded. "When we have gone farther, we will have a council."

"We have enough to carry!" cried a warrior angrily. "If we are to kill him, let us kill him now. He is white, like the others who have lied to us!"

Rod glanced around the hostile faces looking down at him. His eyes paused at sight of one of them. It was the face of a slender boy, staring at him from behind the others. It, too, reflected hostility, yet there was a different look, a terrible uncertainty that was like a deep hurt.

Rod's lips moved: "Shakochee!"

It seemed as if he looked at his friend for hours before the Indian boy thrust forward a shoulder and wormed his way through the crowd. His face was set and stern. He came toward Rod and stood beside him, his flickering shadow falling protectively over the white boy. He raised a hand to speak and the others were quiet.

"I know this Luckmaker!" he said firmly. "We have hunted together long ago. He is my friend."

One of the braves jeered. The others were silent. Only then did Rod see how his own friendship had weighted Shakochee with the disapproval of his people. He understood the young Indian's stern, angry look and his slowness to come forward. Once the two of them had been friends, with no troubles between them. But the war had raised a barrier.

Against the enmity that hung thickly in the air, the old warrior with the steady voice was speaking. "Tell us, Shakochee, what you know about this white boy."

With dignity Shakochee stood straight. In the dancing light he looked a seasoned warrior. Rod noted that he was almost as tall now as himself. The past year had made a difference.

"This Luckmaker has been good to me," Shakochee was saying, his voice taut. "He has helped me and I have helped him. Once he freed me from Sam Ruther, the slave catcher. He does not lie like the others."

The loyal words made Rod's heart warm. But the other Indians were not moved. The old warrior came forward then, and spoke slowly:

"Let us send this white boy to the general at Fort Brooke. He can carry our message. He will say, 'Look no more for the Seminoles. They have gone to their homeland. They never will go to Arkansas.'"

Someone in the crowd grumbled that the white troops would follow them too quickly, and the old man replied in a sharp tone: "It is late. We must hurry. Let Shakochee stay here until dawn. Then he will release this Luck-maker. Come, we must go."

The warriors turned back toward the trail. One of the braves cut down the turkey and toted it to his horse. In a few moments the procession was again under way.

Soon the columns grew spindly, petered out. The forest echoed their fading sounds. The light of the torches died away. Shakochee knelt and cut the rawhide around Rod's wrists and ankles. In the moonlight his face was indistinct.

"Thanks for helping me," said Rod as he got stiffly to his feet.

"It is what I must do."

They looked at each other awkwardly. The enmity still was there, defying the friendship. Shakochee asked, "Where is this man who tied you? Is he near?"

Rod felt a stab of warning. "We'd better hide. He'll be back; soon."

"You have no gun?"

"He took mine."

Shakochee motioned toward a cluster of oaks grown together at the base. "Step into the place between the trunks. It is good hiding. I will cover the trail."

"Lend me your knife," said Rod.

Gravely Shakochee handed him his knife.

The white boy slashed off a long strand of grapevine which he stretched, ankle-high, across the trail.

"It doesn't show in this light," he observed with satisfaction. "If we can trip Galda, he'll be easy to take."

Shakochee nodded without smiling.

Rod gathered more of the vine before he followed his friend into the cleft trunk of the oak. Carefully he cut the strand into two pieces, rolled them into a loose coil, and laid it beside him. "It's stronger than rope," he said.

"This must be a strong man," Shakochee noted.

Rod wasn't sure. "He's lean but he looks tough, like this vine."

Shakochee glanced quickly at Rod. "Is he of the Spanish people? One with a bullet hole in the shoulder of his shirt?"

Rod was surprised. "Yes. Do you know him?"

"I have seen him," replied Shakochee ruefully. "He came to our camp last night, soon after I arrived with Coacoochee. He asked for two slaves."

"Slaves!" exclaimed Rod. "I didn't know he was a slave catcher!"

"Perhaps not," said Shakochee cannily. "Perhaps he only wished to rob us as the others have done. The Negroes he tried to take were born in Suwannee Old Town. They had run away from no one."

"Did he get them?"

Shakochee shook his head, a strange smile on his lips. "Micanopy fooled him. He told him to come back tomorrow."

"I'm glad."

The two words seemed to thaw Shakochee. He said nothing, but his eyes were friendlier as the two boys sat in silence. Far off a wolf howled and an owl whirred beneath the spreading branches of the oaks. Rod had a question he wanted to ask, but he wasn't sure just how to put it. At last he made a halting effort: "I don't understand—and none of the white men will understand—why the Indians left Fort Brooke."

He waited for a reply, but none came.

"Was it because the Negro slaves were taken with General Jesup's permission?"

Shakochee was slow to answer. "Mostly it was because of the slaves," he said at last. "But there were other reasons. Partly it was because . . ." He broke off, listening intently. Nothing echoed in the night air but the cry of whippoorwills and the twanging of a tree frog.

"Partly what?" asked Rod curiously.

"It was said that Indian throats would be cut once the tribes went west."

"That isn't true!" Rod retorted indignantly.

"Osceola and Coacoochee have declared this."

"They were mistaken," Rod argued. "It isn't true. The white men only want the Indians to go west."

Shakochee's voice became morose and bitter. "Seminole say, 'Why should the white man tell me where to go? I was born here, so were my fathers.'"

"There should be room for both Indians and whites," Rod agreed, but in his heart he knew other white men would not say the same.

Chapter 6

The Bribe

Following the Fort Brooke desertion by the Indians, the "press condemned General Jesup without inquiry or investigation."

—John T. Sprague
in *The Florida War*

FOR HOURS the two friends waited in the oak, sometimes sitting in the firmly grown crotch of the trunks to rest themselves, sometimes standing, while Shakochee found a limb across which to level his gun. Rod was hungry but dared not mention food because he knew the Indians' disdain for one who is a slave to his stomach.

There were many alarms. Far away a shot sounded and broke off the down-scale cry of a raccoon. Thinking the gun was Galda's, the boy jerked to attention. Shakochee fingered his rifle and Rod slid his hunting knife in and out of its sheath to be sure it wouldn't stick. But after half an hour of waiting, they decided the hunter had gone another way.

Once they both stiffened as a rabbit screamed. But

Shakochee said quickly, "It is only that an owl is feeding."

When the woods were quiet, they talked in low tones.

"What have you done, Shakochee, since I saw you?" Rod asked.

Shakochee looked straight ahead. The line of his jaw was hard. "I have fought white men."

"And I've fought Indians," acknowledged Rod.

"Were you at Fort Mellon when Coacoochee's warriors came?"

Rod shook his head. "No. Were you with Coacoochee?"

"Yes. I have a scar in my side. See?" Shakochee pointed to a healed-over wound just above the hip bone.

"That's a bad place," observed Rod. "I knew a man who died from being shot there."

"My root saved me," explained the warrior.

"Your root?" questioned Rod, surprised. He recognized the quiet faith in his friend's voice, but he knew of no root with such powers. "What root have you, Shakochee? Something from a medicine bundle?"

"It is of no special bundle," said the Indian. He glanced at his friend as if uncertain how much he should say. "It is another root—one we have just found," he confided. "Hil-lis-waw, it is called. It cures quickly. It will almost bring a man back from death." He reached into his pocket and drew out a gnarled bit of root, not more than two inches long. "See, it looks like this."

Rod peered through the darkness. "May I touch it?"

"Hold it," offered the Indian, "but be careful of it. I

must keep it always. When I die it will go to my children, and they will give it to their children. It must last a long time."

Rod took the root, ran his fingers lightly over it, and held it to his nose, thinking it might be sassafras. It gave forth a faintly acrid odor that matched nothing he ever had known.

"What shape is its leaf?" he asked curiously, as he handed back the root.

"Small and a deep green," explained the Indian, "with edges like a saw."

"Is there a secret about the place it's found?" asked Rod hesitantly, thinking that his mother would like to have some of this root.

"There is no secret," replied the Indian. "But I hunted many days. Others have never seen hil-lis-waw growing. I have shared mine with our band."

"Will it keep them well?"

"We will live long," replied Shakochee firmly.

From the trail to the west came a faint crackle. Both boys were quiet and Rod's hand sought his knife. Then came the soft pad of moccasins and the brush of a body against saplings heavy with new growth.

Neither boy spoke. Shakochee balanced his gun across the tree branch, fitted the butt tightly against his shoulder, and sighted down onto the path. Rod felt for the coil of vine, found it loose and untangled beside him.

The steps came closer, hesitated, came on again. Once more they paused uncertainly.

He's looking for me, Rod thought.

In the quiet of the forest, the steps seemed unnaturally loud. One . . . two . . . three . . . four. Where the trail turned sharply, the Spaniard's shadow appeared, his lean body outlined in the broken shafts of moonlight.

Scarcely breathing, Rod waited. Galda walked slowly, peering from side to side. On he came toward the tree.

When he was only a few steps from the vine, he stopped suddenly, eyes riveted on something to the right. With an abrupt motion he yanked his gun to his shoulder.

Rod's fist contracted against his knife. The chance to catch the trader off guard was gone. Something had alerted him and now he stood below them, gun up and ready to fire.

Silently Rod leaped from the tree crotch. He struck Galda's left shoulder. With a crash the two of them fell, the man's bones crackling weirdly against the ground. His gun jarred from his grasp, and Rod kicked it out of reach.

With all his young energy, the boy tried to pin the wiry Spaniard. But his muscles gradually gave way against the older man's tough strength. Rod's wrist, twisted slowly, burned with red-hot pain. The knife dropped from his fingers. And with a sudden hard wrench of the body, Galda turned them both over and emerged on top.

His hands were fumbling for Rod's throat when Shakochee's voice cut sharply through the darkness. "Galda—
stand up!"

Rod sensed the trader's astonishment as he glanced
toward the oak. At sight of the round gun muzzle trained
on him, his body froze. With reluctance he let his fingers
relax and got slowly to his feet.

"Hands above the head!" snapped Shakochee.

Still watching the gun, the Spaniard raised his arms.
In the moonlight he looked like a skinny scarecrow with
unnaturally black eyes and white eyeballs.

"Tie him, Rod."

Rod scrambled toward the vine, grasped it, and approached the trader. With his free hand he yanked the
man's knife out of its sheath and tossed it beside his rifle.

"Hands behind your back," he ordered.

The Spaniard did not obey. "I do only for him who
has the gun," he said, his voice shaking with pent-up
anger.

Shakochee repeated Rod's order.

Slowly the trader did as told. Rod looped the vine
around his wrists, keeping it tight and knotting it several
times. Galda glared at him and grunted with each jerk.
But when the work was done he suddenly turned to
Shakochee and began to wheedle.

"Why have you turned against me, Semoli?"

The Indian did not answer, and the Spaniard pleaded,
"For the Semoli I have been put in jail."

Still Shakochee did not speak, and a note of anger crept into the man's voice. "I have sold your people powder and guns. For this I am to suffer again?"

"You have tried to steal their slaves, too," said Shakochee gruffly.

Galda was taken aback. But in a moment he began excusing himself, speaking earnestly and with emotion. "I have been made to do this. It was not I who wanted the Semoli's slaves, but the white general. He would kill me if I did not do as he said."

"Don't believe him, Shakochee," protested Rod, indignant at the man's lies. "He wanted those slaves for himself."

"Has he sold powder and guns to the Indians?" asked Shakochee warily.

This was dangerous ground, and Rod knew it. But he answered honestly. "Yes. They put him in jail for it, but he got out."

"Then he is not the Indian's enemy?"

"He's not their friend either!" Rod declared vehemently. "He sold powder to them for the money he could make. He wanted slaves for the same reason."

"I have more powder—and guns," interposed Galda with persuasive softness. "I will give them to you, Semoli, if you set me free."

"He lies!" exclaimed Rod angrily, and was reminded that Galda had made the same outcry that day in Judge Parton's cabin.

"How much powder? How many guns?" asked Shako-chee coldly.

"All I have!"

"Look, Shakochee . . ." interrupted Rod. But his words were unheard.

"Where are they?"

"That I cannot say."

"Where are they?" repeated the Indian roughly.

"They are buried."

"He's lying, Shakochee!" put in Rod. "Can't you see how he hesitates? He has to think of a lie before he can say it."

Shakochee's voice was persistent, ignoring his friend. "Where are these guns buried?"

"That I cannot tell while this—this Rod Wheeler stands by," sputtered the Spaniard. "I cannot give him my secrets. He runs to the white general and tattles."

Rod sought for a powerful argument. He could not, within reason, expect Shakochee to give up powder and guns. Yet something assured the boy that Galda was lying.

"He hasn't anything, Shakochee!" Rod burst out. "He's just trying to get away—can't you see it? He'll lead you to some far-off spot and then you'll find there isn't any powder—or guns either."

"Then he shall die," said Shakochee matter-of-factly.

"Why do you argue with this white boy?" asked Galda, nettled at the young warrior's words. "Why does he urge

you to do this and you do it—to do that and you do it?
Are you not a man who can think for himself?"

The taunt made an impression. "I am a man," replied
Shakochee with towering dignity. "You will be surprised
to see, Zade Galda, that my gun is as deadly as that of an
old warrior. If there is no powder, or guns, where you say,
my rifle shall speak and you will be quiet for a long time."

Shocked at Shakochee's implied acceptance of the offer,
Rod said quickly, "I'll go with you, Shakochee."

The Indian's voice was thin and sharp. "You, Luckmaker, must go to the fort. You carry a message. I have
promised."

Rod stared at his friend. It was true. Shakochee had
promised, and Rod had been glad to accept the terms
offered for his freedom. Now he must live up to them.
Yet he was sure Galda had no guns. And he wanted, if
humanly possible, to return the Spaniard to jail.

"Look, Shakochee," he pleaded. "You've got to take me.
When General Jesup discovers the Indians have gone,
he'll have soldiers combing these woods all around the
Bay. They'll be shooting at anybody that looks like an
Indian. The mainland'll be about as safe for you as Fort
Brooke. If I . . ."

"He speaks for himself!" interrupted Galda.

"If I help you find that powder and the guns, can I go?"
urged Rod.

Shakochee seemed to waver, and Galda spoke up swiftly,
his voice smooth as silk. "It is not on the mainland that the

guns are hidden. Where I take you there is no danger. You will not need this white friend."

"Must we cross water then?" asked Shakochee in surprise.

The trader hesitated. "Yes, we must cross water."

Rod rejoiced silently. Luck had turned his way again. Aloud, he said, "I have a boat, Shakochee. It's near here, in the mangroves, along the bayou. I'll take you to the guns."

Galda was silent, stunned.

"Come, Luckmaker," agreed Shakochee, starting to crawl out of the tree. "We will use your boat. Turn to the south, Galda."

Even in the dim moonlight, Rod could see the bafflement on the trader's face. The man moved slowly toward the south trail, Shakochee close behind.

Rod picked up the rifle Galda had dropped and was elated to discover it was his own. He touched the flint and frizzen, fingered the trigger and found them just the same as always. With a flip of his wrist, he retrieved the Spaniard's knife, stuck it in his belt and followed the others through the woods.

His thoughts were busy as he led the way toward the mangroves where *The Pelican* was anchored. Could he capture Galda without hurting Shakochee? Would Shakochee shoot him if he made such an attempt? How would it all turn out?

But abruptly his questions were answered by his own good sense. He would have to wait until Shakochee released the Spaniard, then capture him. That way the Indian's promise would be honored, yet Rod could do his duty as he saw it.

It would be a dangerous move, tricky as touching fire to gunpowder. For this time, if Galda gained the upper hand, he would not be stingy.

Chapter 7

Cockroach Key

"They (the Indians) throughout the whole war, conducted affairs with a bold and resolute hand. Every engagement proved their superiority in bush-fighting; and it is no disparagement to our troops to say, 'the war was only a succession of disasters'; for Florida with its many advantages for Indian warfare, offered nothing but obstacles to the operations of our troops."
—Journal of Jacob R. Motte,
in *Journey into Wilderness*, 1953

THE EASTERN sky was silvery, like the inside of a clamshell, when the two boys and their prisoner emerged from the bayou mouth. The bay was a gently undulating sheet of gray.

"Which way?" asked Shakochee.

Galda nodded to the south.

Rod rowed out beyond the shallows toward smoother water. In a few minutes the ebbing tide had seized *The Pelican* and was pulling it swiftly past shore.

Three was a crowd in the small boat, and its gunwales lay close to the water. Galda sat in the stern, his wrists still bound. Rod had taken the center seat and Shakochee

76

was cross-legged on the bottom of the craft, his gun covering their prisoner.

Rod wished he could have sent word to his pa that he was going down-bay. He was worried, too, that his father would be hunting him.

"I think I know this place to which Galda takes us," said Shakochee suddenly. "We Indians call it Place of the Dead."

"Place of the Dead," repeated Rod, puzzled and repelled by the name. "I never heard of any such island."

Galda had been silent. Now he spoke up, his voice almost friendly. "You are right, Semoli. That is the Indian name. There I have guns. You will see. I gladly give them to help the Semoli in their fight."

Rod felt uneasy. He still wasn't sure that the Spaniard would fail to persuade Shakochee of his friendship. But there was no reading the Indian's face. It was smooth and masklike.

As Rod's oars stirred the water, they left a trail of phosphorescence, like stars flashing dimly in a night sky. But when the sun brightened the horizon, the glow vanished and only white wavelets marked the boat's course.

"Good thing I brought my worm shovel," observed Rod. "I just put it in the boat yesterday. We'll need something for digging."

"There is much shell on this island," Shakochee rejoined, "and digging will not be easy."

To Rod's surprise, the Spaniard spoke reassuringly.

"The guns lie near the top," he announced. "If you let me use the shovel, I can get them out quickly."

"That is good," said Shakochee.

Rod dissented within himself. Galda would get no shovel or any other kind of weapon, crude though it might be, in his hands. Nor would he be unbound, if Rod had anything to say about it. He wondered what the Spaniard planned to do when they reached the island. Somehow, the white boy didn't think Galda wanted a fight, with two rifles against Rod's old worm shovel. What was the fellow's plan?

Rod looked at Shakochee and the Indian's answering glance seemed to say, "We must beware of this Zade Galda. He is full of tricks."

Aloud the Seminole spoke softly: "You, Luckmaker, must go ashore first and make sure there is no one. I will hold the Spaniard."

The sun was shining through the pine forest now, a golden-pink ball that cast delicate shadows over the water. From the shore came the early morning tumult of hungry birds and the strident calls of the gulls. A slow-flapping pelican wheeled out toward the boat, turned heavily and sailed back toward shore, plopping suddenly into the water as he sighted a minnow.

Beneath his excitement, Rod was aware that he, too, was now very hungry. At home his family would be eating breakfast—oatmeal that had cooked all night in the Dutch oven or pancakes fried in the iron skillet.

"How many guns have you?" Shakochee asked abruptly of the prisoner.

For the first time Galda seemed uneasy. "I am not sure," he replied. "I have buried them in a canvas. I am not sure how many."

Rod did not take the talk seriously. There were no guns, he was certain. But he was alarmed as to Galda's plan when they reached the island.

For hours they rowed silently. The sun's heat began to reflect from the water. Pelicans settled lazily on dead trees at the bay's edge, and in a shallow cove Rod saw a long line of flamingoes, their pinkish-red feathers bright spots of color against the narrow beach.

Along the horizon a mound of land began to rise, slowly at first, but growing quickly into a humpy island of sand and shell, with spots of green vegetation and clumps of cabbage palms. In the morning light it glistened faintly.

"We are drawing close to the Place of the Dead," said Shakochee, his eyes on Galda.

"Si, Semoli," Galda agreed.

It seemed to Rod that the man's eyes searched restlessly over the Place of the Dead. Aloud Rod remarked, "We call this Cockroach Key. I've passed it lots of times when I was fishing with Pa."

"But it is a place of the dead," said Shakochee with dignity. "Many are buried there, in long mounds. Other mounds hold things they have used in life. Have you never stepped ashore?"

"No," confessed Rod. "It looks as if there's nothing on it."

"No living thing now," agreed Shakochee. "No Indian goes here. We do not dishonor the graves."

Rod guided the rowboat to shore at the north end of Cockroach Key, and Shakochee leaped out onto the sand, sending an army of fiddler crabs scuttling for their holes. He held his gun on the Spaniard, while Rod pulled the boat high and dry.

"I will stay here while you look over the island," Shakochee said cautiously. "Look everywhere, for I do not trust this trader."

Rod was pleased with the last words, for he himself felt the man about as trustworthy as the big sharks that sometimes drifted into the bay. And he was glad to know that Galda's friendliness hadn't softened Shakochee.

Gun in hand, he climbed the slope of the first mound, his moccasins crunching in the broken shell. This must be a refuse heap, he thought, for it was dotted with fragments of pottery. At the crest of the hill he paused to survey the lonely droplet of land. Only a few acres, it hardly seemed an island at all—more like a cluster of humps rearing out of the bay, with no greenery except palms, bunches of saw palmetto, and sea oats. Nothing else that would conceal either man or beast.

He turned with the idea of motioning to Shakochee, but changed his mind. He would examine that palmetto and go to the top of the second mound before deciding that the place was deserted.

He waded down the refuse slope and up to the crest of the burial mound. Several times he glimpsed the shiny gray of fossil shark's teeth but did not pause to pick them up.

The second hill was larger than the first, and Rod strode toward the clump of palms at its top. An osprey taking flight and a solitary pelican on a stump near the south end of the island convinced him that the place was empty, but he probed the undergrowth with his moccasin and went to the far edge of the key.

Back at the first hill he motioned the others to come.

"Get up. Walk!" he heard Shakochee say, with a threatening jab of the rifle toward his prisoner.

Hands still tied behind him, Galda struggled to his feet, stepped out of the boat and started up the hill. He walked quickly, as if he were eager to find the guns. Rod watched him, expecting trouble. Without glancing at the boy, Galda crossed the hill, plodded down its slope and up the next, Shakochee and Rod close behind.

All three came to a halt at the top of the second mound, while the Spaniard gazed across the island. "It is strange to me," he faltered. "I have not been here for a while."

"But you have guns here," Shakochee reminded, his eyes stern.

"Si, si—I have guns," the man replied, adding vaguely,

"they are near here. Untie me and I will test the earth to find them."

"You will test only your memory," said Shakochee. "If you have guns here, you can find them better that way."

Galda's voice reflected his quick anger. "I only ask to be untied so I can dig," he flung back. "I must uncover the guns."

"Rod will dig," said Shakochee shortly, handing the shovel to his friend.

The Spaniard's temper glowed in his face. "Many times this Rod Wheeler has caused me trouble. Now he is to dig! While he is here, I will not say where the guns are planted."

Shakochee raised his rifle slowly, sighted along its barrel toward the man's chest. "You will say. Now."

Galda's eyes flicked nervously across the island, as if he were looking for help. "There," he said, nodding toward a palmetto clump that reared its prickly fans beneath three cabbage palms.

A cold finger raced up Rod's spine as he glimpsed a bleached skull deep in the scrub. But a second look told him it was only the head bones of some small animal, probably a raccoon.

He glanced at Shakochee. "Let's hobble Galda before I start digging."

But the Indian shook his head impatiently. "My gun

is pointed at his heart. If he tries to escape, I will shoot. I am not fooled by his talk of friendship."

Rod approached the palmettos, pushed aside their fans, and thrust the edge of the shovel into the earth. "Is this the spot?"

The Spaniard nodded silently.

Rod drove the blade deep into the ground and threw aside a shovelful of sand and shell. In a few minutes he had made a hole two feet square and about the same depth. He halted.

"I thought you said the guns lie near the top," he reminded Galda.

To his surprise both the prisoner and Shakochee were looking at something out in the bay, toward the ocean. Rod looked, too. A fishing boat with two men was approaching the key.

"Ahoy!" cried someone in the boat.

Rod's first impulse was to answer "Ahoy." But he hesitated.

"Ahoy!" came the cry again.

Still uncertain whether to answer, Rod looked at Shakochee. The Indian was tensed, ready to run. These white men would take him back to Fort Brooke if they found him here, he knew that. Galda's face had brightened and his sharp eyes were fixed on the Indian. Although Shakochee's gun still held him captive, he was waiting for a break.

In the fishing boat a man raised his rifle. Its low groan sounded across the water. The bullet struck Rod's gun where it stood against a palm and slapped it down into the sand.

Before he could move or think, Shakochee's gun replied. In the bay, one of the boat's sails spanked sharply. In the same instant Galda darted, swift-legged, across the top of the mound and down its eastern slope, shouting, "Help me! Help me from Semoli!"

Rod grabbed for his gun, saw that the mechanism was bent, and turned to Shakochee. The Indian was reloading with feverish haste. He guessed at the powder load, rammed in a ball, and spilled more powder into the pan. In one swift motion he raised gun to shoulder, sighted and fired.

The Spaniard had reached the narrow beach and was splashing through the shallows toward the boat. At the rifle shot he stumbled and fell forward. His body half sank beneath the water. A ribbon of red flowed into the blue. Then the tide seized his body and began to pull it toward the mouth of the bay.

Again Shakochee was reloading. Rod grasped him by the arm. "No!"

For a brief second, Shakochee stared strangely at his friend, as if he were angry with him, too. Then suddenly he stuffed the bullet back into his shot pouch and ran with Rod across the mounds to *The Pelican*. They leaped in, each grabbed an oar and set to paddling. In half a minute they were scooting across channel.

"Head for the creek!" cried Rod.

They turned the rowboat farther upshore to where a creek emptied into the bay, and dug their oars hard into the water.

The fishermen did not try to follow. They had floated close to Zade Galda. One of them reached over the side and brought up the limp body. With a heave he dragged it into the boat.

"Galda looks dead," said Rod, his breath so short he could hardly speak.

Shakochee was calm. "It is good. He was a bad man to both our people. You have said it truly."

They reached the sheltering creek and turned up it. Slowly an arm of land reached out and shut the fishing boat from view. They did not slow down, but sent the craft skimming upstream. Those men must not find Shakochee. To them he was just an Indian who had shot and killed a white man. If they caught him, there would be no trial, nor even any chance to explain.

A long way upcreek, they began to move more slowly. The channel had narrowed and in places the woods came down thickly to the water.

"Here!" said Shakochee at last. "Here is a good place. We can hide the boat in this swampy spot, in the saw grass."

Rod shook his head stubbornly. "I'm going farther. You can catch up with your friends lots sooner. I'll come out to the bay after dark."

"Will they not find you?"

"No. I'll watch for them."

"You are sure?"

"I'm sure, Shakochee."

"Good then."

They paddled for a long way, until Shakochee again called for a stop. The woods were dense and would make good hiding. Rod did not feel afraid for his friend.

He headed the boat toward shore and waited while Shakochee picked up his gun and leaped out of the craft.

"Here I leave you, Luckmaker," the Indian said, pausing for a moment on the bank. "I think you will have no more trouble with Zade Galda."

"Good-bye, Shakochee."

"Good-bye."

As the Indian vanished into the woods, Rod felt a lump of loneliness rise in his throat. Ashamed of his weakness, he sat down to wait for darkness.

Chapter 8

The Fly-Up-the-Creek

"The citizens, harassed and plundered and deceived as they had been, from time to time by their (the Indians) professions of friendship and capitulations, and seeing no end to the conflict, took the field, resolved to put to death every Indian that fell into their hands."

—John T. Sprague
in *The Florida War*

AT FORT BROOKE things were in an uproar. Detachments had been sent into the woods to find the missing Indians. A few who had been caught and brought back were being held under strictest guard.

The seven hundred had split into small bands and were scattering through the country, making capture difficult.

Residents of Tampa talked of nothing but the treaty violation and charged the army with carelessness for letting the Indians get away so easily. The soldiers were full of quiet argument among themselves, most of them blaming General Jesup for the debacle.

"It means the war again," said a discouraged soldier. "Just when I was sure we'd finished with this one. Got a touch of fever and I'm anxious to be out of here."

"The Indians never intended to go west," said another bitterly. "They've got new clothes now, are fed up, and their crops have had time to grow. They're ready for war again."

Others said the general had made a mistake in allowing the sailing date to be postponed while the Seminoles waited for relatives or friends.

"Where the general really was wrong," remarked a third cannily, "was in letting those slave catchers come in and carry off the Indians' slaves. It looked like a change in the treaty."

Rod went at once to the fort and reported his recent adventure to General Jesup himself. The general's eyes were shrunken and dull from his sleepless vigil while the hunt was on, but he listened eagerly.

"Indians headed southeast, you say? Just what we figured."

When he heard about the expedition to dig up guns, he shook his head. "You should have brought the prisoner direct to the fort, Rod."

"Sir, I was in a peculiar position. I guess you'd say I was Shakochee's prisoner myself."

The general's eyebrows rose, but he said nothing more. He was too tired and harassed to care much about one Indian, or even about the escaped Spaniard.

"You're right that Galda is dead," he said, leafing through his official reports. "Two fishermen came in yesterday and said they had dragged a body from the channel there and buried it on the mainland. Undoubtedly your man."

Rod breathed a deep sigh of relief. "Thank you, sir."

As he left the fort, he felt a weight had been taken off his mind. Zade was dead. He had been buried. Rod's own part in the incident was now reported and he had taken a mild rebuke from the general. The episode was closed.

Like the army commander, Mr. Wheeler had shown disapproval of his son's journey to Cockroach Key.

"Two boys are no match for a man like Galda," he said gravely. "It could easily have been you or Shakochee who was fished out of the channel."

"It could, sir," Rod admitted.

"Next time think twice before you pitch off on such a trip."

"I will, sir."

Rod still hoped that his father might return to the farm, and brought the matter up the same morning as they were cleaning a turtle together.

"Will there be war again, Pa?"

"Bound to be, son."

"There's no chance, then, of going back to the farm?"

"Not yet."

"They caught some of the Indians, you know," Rod persisted, unwilling to give up hope. "Just brought in another bunch when I was over at the fort. They're being shipped west. Don't you think the others might change their minds and come in?"

"Not now."

Rod looked moodily at the brown shell of the gopher turtle. "I guess John Fox will be putting a notch on the other side of his gun."

"A notch?" his father asked curiously. "What for?"

Rod explained about Fox's notched gun. "Now it's the Indians have broken a treaty. I guess he'll be cutting a piece out on their side."

"Most likely he will," agreed Mr. Wheeler.

It was almost two days before Rod felt it safe to return to Cockroach Key. He did not expect to find treasure, but merely to get his worm shovel, which in the excitement they had left on the island. During his wait he repaired the frizzen of his gun and tried it out thoroughly.

Early one morning he finished his chores, put a bottle of water and some corn bread in the boat, and again rowed south.

Ever since his trip to Cockroach he had thought about the glittery little hump of sand rising out of the bay, and wondered idly why Galda had taken them to that spot. It seemed unlikely that the man had expected a fishing boat to come past. It had just happened, and Galda had tried to seize his advantage. The fact that the men had reported their encounter at the fort indicated that they were honest fishermen on their way home from deeper waters.

He made the trip even more quickly than before and beached *The Pelican* at the north end of the key. Today he noticed a great many things that had escaped him when he and Shakochee were guarding the Spaniard. On his way up the first mound, he picked up a huge shark tooth embedded in the shell debris. The point had been filed sharp, and he recognized it as the stabbing end of a harpoon. He polished it against his shirt, examined it again, and then tucked it carefully into his pocket.

There was lots of broken pottery sticking out of the first mound, all of it crude and without design. He found a few shell hammers and a bone arrowhead.

At the crest of the second mound he paused and looked around him. The place appeared just as deserted as before. Under the fiery sun of late morning it was oppressively hot, and Rod wished he had brought a bigger supply of water.

There was his shovel, lying beside the hole he had dug. He picked it up and leaned on its handle, looking at the little excavation and wondering if he should dig further.

Just on the chance that Galda might actually have had something buried, Rod began digging, enlarged the hole and went down several feet deeper. Nothing appeared but the same sand and bits of shell that seemed to make up the island.

He gave up, leaned on his shovel again and wiped his perspiring forehead. His thoughts were so far away that he failed to notice a faint rattling of palmetto fans as a fly-up-the-creek cried shrilly in the palm clump. But as the call was repeated, it bored through Rod's absorption. He ducked into the scrub, where he crouched, warily cocking his gun and looking for an enemy.

From his hiding spot he could see almost all of the island. The sand still glittered in the sun. The palm fans stirred faintly in the breeze. Only this small patch of scrub could hide anything bigger than a rabbit.

Again came the heron's cry, sending a cold prickle up Rod's spine. He knew the call was not that of a real fly-up-the-creek, which is a shy bird, fearful of humans and apt to stand motionless if seen. And the sound came from less than a dozen feet away in the same area of scrub that hid Rod himself.

He swung his gun muzzle in that direction and waited.

"Luckmaker, it is I," came a voice that sounded strangely like Shakochee's and yet did not. "Look under the scrub."

Rod grinned shamefacedly, put down his gun, and walked toward the sound. On the far side of the palmettos he found his friend. The Indian was pale and there was pain in his dark eyes, even though his mouth smiled. One thigh was bound with a bloody piece of calico.

"What happened?" asked Rod, his throat tight with pity.

"I met soldiers," said Shakochee, glancing toward the bandaged leg. "It was as you said. The mainland is filled with them."

Rod nodded. "How'd you get back—did you swim?"

"I was lucky. The tide was slack. But my gun is still on the other side."

Rod noted the boy's dry lips. "I'll get you some water."

He trotted back to the boat, got both the water and the corn bread, and returned to Shakochee. The Indian refused the offer of help and raised himself on one elbow while he drank, slowly at first, then a little faster, until he had finished half the bottle.

"Good," he said, his eyes grateful.

"Can you eat?"

"I am hungry."

Rod handed him the corn bread. Shakochee ate it all, slowly but with relish.

"Let me look at your leg," suggested Rod, when the food was gone. "If it's bad I can get some medicine from my mother. She doctors lots of folks."

"No," replied Shakochee emphatically, covering the bandage with his hand. "I have eaten a little of my new root, and the wound is healing. I needed food and water. Now I will be well."

"Let me see."

Shakochee rolled back the calico and revealed the skin near the bullet hole. Rod touched it gently. There was little soreness and he agreed that the flesh was healing.

"May I take off the bandage?"

Shakochee shook his head. "No. It is good, I tell you. The root does not fail."

"Then I'll hunt more food."

Anxiously Rod thought over the things he could get for Shakochee. Coon oysters were plentiful on the mangrove roots, and they were good-tasting, though small. With the shark's-tooth harpoon, he could spear a fish. If he went over to the mainland, he could get game of some kind, but it would take a lot longer and the sound of his rifle might draw soldiers.

He decided to try the harpoon. He made a handle for it from the center stalk of a palm fan, binding it to the shark's tooth with a bit of palm fiber and railroad vine. It took him half an hour to spear a sea trout from the boat, but he felt the effort worth it, for Shakochee would surely enjoy this fine-tasting fish.

Before he beached the boat again, he poled alongside the mangroves and pried off several dozen oysters. Then, with his bounty, he returned to the Indian.

Shakochee was better already. He smiled at sight of the fish, and showed Rod where he had gathered dried fans to lay a fire.

Rod drew out his flint and worked patiently until he ignited the tinder-dry fans. In a few minutes the flames were crackling high. While he worked, Shakochee had prepared the fish, wrapped it in a green leaf, and laid it on the ashes.

They set the oysters beside the fire, where the shells opened slowly and the tender meat was cooked in a short time. The two boys ate them along with the trout.

"Many times you have proved my friend," said the Indian boy solemnly as he took his last bite of the fish.

Rod looked away and said nothing. He was grateful for

Shakochee's thanks, which oftener were expressed by deeds than by words. Best of all, it seemed now as if the barrier between them was gone.

As the fire gleamed low and died back, Rod told the Indian about digging for the guns and finding nothing. "I guess you saw me," he added.

"Yes," said Shakochee. "But I was not surprised that Galda lied to us."

"Galda is dead," Rod told him. He related his talk with General Jesup concerning the two fishermen, and Shakochee nodded, apparently not surprised by this news either.

"I'm sorry we got mixed up with him," said Rod, as he scooped sand onto the embers of the fire. "I feel it was my fault. You didn't even know him and now you're the one who has a bullet wound."

"I am not sad," observed Shakochee. "For what a man does, he does. He chooses what seems to him good, and abides by the outcome."

The two of them sat there talking until the sun hung low in the sky. Rod told Shakochee about the silver chest which the Spaniard had received from the Indians. His friend eyed him curiously. "I have heard of this chest. It is well known among our people. The face on it is the face of a king—not of our nation, but of nations to the west, over deep water."

He paused. Rod said nothing. He felt it was not good manners to be curious now, for Shakochee was telling him a secret of his own people.

"The box came to us on the tide, floating in with a wrecked ship. At first it was filled with gold, but my people have much need of money and the gold was spent. I did not know until now that the chest had been traded to Galda."

Rod's thought went back to the day he had strained his eyes to see the odd chest. So it was foreign, and made of real silver. More than ever he was curious as to its whereabouts.

Aloud he said, "The face—do the Indians hold the box dear because of the face?"

Shakochee shook his head. "He was not a king of our people."

The sparks of the fire were all black. The tide was turning. It was time to leave. Rod stood up. "Good-bye, Shakochee. My father expects me home. I'll come tomorrow. What shall I bring you?"

Shakochee sat up quickly. "Row me to the mainland," he urged. "I am well enough now."

Rod was startled. "With that leg? No, sir. You've got to stay here till I get you fed up a little."

"I am well," repeated the Indian stubbornly. He struggled to his feet. "I will go."

Rod put out a detaining hand. "Stay here," he repeated gently. "A detachment of soldiers was sent south this morning. They'll be searching over there, in the scrub and in every hollow log. Stay here."

Shakochee hesitated, but said darkly, "I do not like this place that Zade Galda brought us to. I only came to hide."

"Then hide a little longer."

"I cannot stay."

Rod saw that it was no use to argue. Shakochee's mind was made up. Yet it was plainly wrong to put his friend ashore where so many white men were hunting Indians. He thought of a compromise.

"If I bring my boat back tonight," he said slowly, "will you wait here for me? I'll take you to the mainland—farther down the coast, where you won't meet any soldiers. I'll row you as far out of the bay as it's safe to go in a small boat. Will you wait?"

Shakochee's face relaxed. "I will wait."

Chapter 9

Shakochee's Gift

"We are attempting, for the first time, the solution of the difficult problem of transferring a savage and a warlike people from one widespread wilderness to another. In every preceding instance of the emigration of an Indian nation, our population had been pressing upon them, and crowding them out of their positions, before any effort had been made by the government to remove them; and the Indians had themselves become sensible of the necessity for removing, long before they had taken up the line of march."

—Major General Thomas S. Jesup
on Oct. 24, 1837

ROD ROWED home as quickly as the heavy oars and thick-timbered boat would take him. He was uncertain just how his father would feel about this whole venture, but he hoped he would understand.

It had been dark for a long time, but the family still was sitting around the fire when Rod entered the cabin on Tampa Bay. Only the glowing embers lighted their faces, which were quiet and thoughtful. Ma had been mending, his brother Hughie had just finished cleaning his gun,

Aunt Cele was dozing, head fallen forward on her chest, and Uncle Ace and Pa were talking in low tones.

They looked up as Rod entered.

"Thank goodness!" exclaimed his mother, stitching harder than ever on a pair of worn moccasins. "We'd all begun to worry about you again."

"What took you so long?" his father asked.

"Something happened, Pa—I had to help a fellow."

"Somebody hurt?" asked Mrs. Wheeler quickly, for she was always ready to help.

"Yes, but he's better. Besides, he's a long way from here. Pa, could I talk to you alone?"

"Why, yes, son."

Mr. Wheeler got up from the hide-bottom chair and followed Rod outside into the night. The salt-edged air was cool, and from the bay came the splash of leaping fish. Now that it was time to ask his father about the night's trip, Rod was uncertain. Down there, on the island with Shakochee, it had seemed a necessary and logical thing. But as he faced his father, all the practical objections rose before him, and he hesitated.

"Pa," he began haltingly, "Shakochee is down on Cockroach Key with a bullet in his leg."

Mr. Wheeler's forehead wrinkled in a faint frown. "Is he badly hurt?"

"A ball in the thigh. He's better, though."

"Good."

"I want to go back and row him over to the mainland."

Mr. Wheeler did not reply at once. Still frowning, he made patterns in the sand with one moccasined foot, looked at the sky and again at the sand. "Who shot him?"

"A soldier—hunting for the Indians who deserted."

"Did Shakochee shoot back? Was any white man wounded or hurt?"

"He didn't say, Pa."

"Son, it would better if he could take care of himself. Can't he swim over?"

In the dim light Rod searched his father's face. But he could not tell if the man strongly disapproved or if he was considering the scheme. "Shakochee's too weak," the boy explained. "He's too bad even to put him off across from Cockroach. I'd row him down the coast toward the mouth of the bay, far as I could, and leave him where he wouldn't be found."

Rod hesitated. "I'm afraid if I don't go back tonight he'll try to swim to shore."

"Tonight! You didn't say you wanted to go tonight, son."

"Yes, Pa. I can't take him across in daytime, it's too dangerous. I promised I'd come back tonight."

"You promised?"

"Yes."

Mr. Wheeler was silent for a moment, then he nodded gravely. "If you promised, you must go. But it's a dangerous thing you're undertaking, Rod. Want me to go with you?"

Rod's heart warmed at the words. It was just as he had known. His pa was fair, clean through. "I'm not afraid to go alone," he replied.

"Go then," said the older man. "It's better if I stay out of it. If a boy helps a friend, it's understood. A grownup has more trouble. Wars and laws and treaties get us pretty mixed up sometimes."

"I'll be going then."

"Wait. Let your mother fix you some supper."

"No, Pa. I'd rather leave before she knows. She might say wait till tomorrow."

The older man smiled faintly. "You're right. She would. Wait here—I'll step inside and get you something."

In a few minutes he was back with a basket of food. He handed it to Rod and went to rummage in the lean-to, returning with a lantern and an empty jug.

"I'll fill this with water while you go down to the boat. Sit in the stern and let me row."

"I thought you didn't want to go," protested Rod.

"I'll row you down the shore a ways, while you eat. You can let me off and I'll walk back."

Rod was pleased. He would have liked his father's company for the whole trip, but he respected the older man's reason for not going.

He tucked the parcel under his arm and took the lantern. Down at the shore he pushed the boat into the shallows and drew up the anchor rock. In a few minutes his father appeared out of the dark, set the water jug in the boat, and climbed in.

No one paid any attention to them as they rowed out into the bay. They passed a fishing boat, draped with nets and dimly lighted fore and aft. And at the fort on the point they could see soldiers sitting around a smudge fire, smoking their pipes and talking before time to turn in.

Mr. Wheeler guided the boat along shore until he had gone about two miles below the cabin, where he grounded the craft and stepped out. Rod had finished a portion of the food—there was plenty for both him and Shakochee—and was ready to take over.

"Be careful, son," Mr. Wheeler warned. "The soldiers are still busy rounding up Indians. They're planning to ship out every one of them they can lay their hands on. And while we think of Shakochee as a boy, he's a warrior to them."

"I'll watch out, Pa," Rod promised.

"Good-bye, then."

"Good-bye."

Rod took up the oars. He dipped them gently in the glassy, moon-silvered shallows and kept close to shore. For a long time he stroked southward, watching the dark vegetation of the mainland glide past. It was late when he saw Cockroach Key loom before him, its mounds black under the low moon.

He grounded the boat at the north end of the island and drew it far up on the sand so that lapping waves would not set it awash. Then he climbed the mounds and headed toward Shakochee's hiding spot.

His heart gave a big thump as he looked down into the palmettos where Shakochee had lain. The place was empty. There was the indentation of the Indian's body. Wild thoughts of roving soldiers from the fort, of Shakochee beating his strength out against the channel current, darted through Rod's head. He had come too late.

A mischievous chuckle sounded behind him. Rod whirled. There, flexing his muscles in the dim light, as if he were ready for a long race, was Shakochee.

"My root has cured me quickly," he called.

He walked to Rod and showed him the wound. Even in the semi-darkness, Rod could see that the leg was healing well.

"It looks good," he admitted, with a grudging admiration for the powers of the root.

"I am well," insisted Shakochee.

"Come then, we'll row south."

Shakochee nodded agreement. "But first we must get my gun from the mainland."

"Do you know the exact spot?"

"Yes."

Rod led the way to the boat, pushed off and stroked across to the wooded shore. They found the gun without difficulty and moved back into the channel for the journey south. While Rod rowed, Shakochee ate the rest of the food from the basket. Waves plucked at the prow of the boat and made phosphorescent ripples where the oars churned the water. Occasionally a fish leaped, and at the mouth of a bayou, Rod heard the chuffing snort of alligators.

"When this tide changes we'll go lots faster," Rod observed.

Gradually the pressure of water against the prow grew less, as the tide moved outward. The shore line unreeled more quickly and rowing was easy. Past little bays and sandspits they hurried, with always the pines, palms or hammocks making a dim blot in the background.

Cockroach Key faded out of sight and the outlines of a larger island crept into view.

"This is a strange island to me," remarked Rod. "Do you know it?"

"Yes," replied Shakochee. "I have been there. Put me ashore a little beyond. I can find my people soon."

The island loomed bigger. In the luminous veil of light that preceded the morning sun, the earth took on a hazy glory, its lush growth of oaks, magnolias and palms acquiring detail under the brightening sky. As the craft came near the key, Rod guided the boat out of the channel and stroked close to the mainland, looking for a place to land.

The sun was bursting over the trees when *The Pelican* ground ashore in a shallow cove. Rod reached out a hand to help Shakochee, but the Indian laughingly ignored it and leaped from the boat by himself.

Instead of running into the woods, as Rod had expected, Shakochee remained standing beside him.

"Here."

Surprised, Rod reached for the tiny object that the young brave held out. It was a piece of wood, hardly larger than a pea. The white boy looked at it curiously, not understanding.

"It is some of the root," said Shakochee. "Even the smallest piece, steeped in water to make a tea, will bring a man back almost from the dead. I did not steep it, but chewed a bit. You see how it has worked."

Rod stared at the particle, hardly trusting himself to speak. It was a fragment of the root—Shakochee's most precious possession, a gift of life. He did not know how to thank his friend.

"I'll use it," he promised. "And I'll remember that you gave it to me."

Chapter 10

St. Augustine

At St. Augustine they "drilled every day in use of the rifle and in the afternoon again until sunset they practiced double quick extensions through the pine barrens, forwarding and rallying skirmishers over bogs and brakes . . . firing by file, one man to draw the Indian from behind the tree and the other to shoot him."

—*A Sketch of the Seminole War*
by a Lieutenant of the
Left Wing, 1836

ROD HAD been in St. Augustine for three days. They were filled with adventure, for he had never seen such a city. Compared to the forest-girdled farm of his boyhood and the crowded military camp at Fort Brooke, it was sophisticated and strange, a jumble of civilizations that had begun almost three hundred years before when Pedro Menéndez de Avilés took possession of land along Matanzas Bay.

The houses were mostly of coquina rock, quarried on offshore Anastasia Island and crowned with the red tile roofs of old Spain. But some heavy-beamed residences betrayed their English origin, and Rod often heard English voices in the streets.

Sometimes, when morning drills were over, he walked along the shore and looked out over the opal-flecked bay. To the left he could see old Fort Marion, crouched on the shore like a bulky sea monster washed up by the waves, its ancient pachyderm walls spotted with lichens, its slotted parapet menacing the pass to the ocean.

When he was off duty, he wandered up and down the city's narrow streets, jostled by the crowds, for the town was near to bursting with refugees. Its grassy plaza was clogged with soldiers' tents, but the townspeople didn't seem to mind, for now that the Indian war had been renewed, they feared attack and thought the army would protect them.

It was almost three months since the seven hundred Indians had deserted Fort Brooke, and new armed forces were ready to march against the Seminoles. There had been skirmishes during the summer and an attempt to negotiate again at Fort King. Although the effort failed, Chief Cohadjo had promised to surrender and bring in the Negroes belonging to his people.

Most of the settlers who had been so optimistic last spring over the coming peace had again left their farms and were bearing arms. They were silent now about the war. The less said the better.

Rod, as part of General Hernandez' volunteer forces, was quartered in a tent with Hart and John Fox. The three had enlisted together and had come across the state only a few days before.

On his way Rod often thought with a twinge of excitement about the painting in his pocket. The girl lived in St. Augustine, he felt sure. He would meet her there.

At first he believed it would be easy to find her—as it would have been in a little village like Tampa. But the size of St. Augustine and its swarms of people made him feel like a shelled pea among hundreds of other peas.

He tried roaming up and down the narrow streets that ran, like shady lanes, between the high-fronted buildings, hoping he would see her. But as that hope faded, he determined to find another way.

With misgivings he showed the painting again to Hart and John Fox. Fox shook his head and Hart said, "Haven't seen her."

"Girls are scarce," added John Fox, "and she's a pretty one. You'd better get a swallow-tailed coat and a haircut if you want to make an impression on her."

Rod flushed. "I don't want to make an impression. I just want to return the picture and to thank her."

Hart reached for the painting and took a long look. "This girl doesn't care about swallow-tailed coats," he announced emphatically. "She'll like Rod the way he is."

Rod was grateful, but still embarrassed. He took the picture back and stuck it deep inside his shirt, near Shakochee's precious root.

"Ask some of the tradesmen about her," Fox suggested,

more practically. "They know all the old residents. One of them could tell you who she is—if she really lives here. That name you showed us doesn't mean a thing. It might be the artist's signature."

Rod wanted to put an end to the discussion of Dolly, so he left the tent and again walked through the streets of the town. He knew John Fox was right in suggesting that he consult one of the tradespeople. But he hesitated. If he showed the picture, everyone would think he liked the girl. Fox had caught on instantly—so had Hart—and it was a secret Rod hated to admit even to himself.

Perhaps if he explained that he had found the painting and wanted to return it, they wouldn't suspect his interest. On the other hand, they might want to take back the picture themselves. Then he never would have a chance to see the girl.

After considerable walking and thinking, he decided to make inquiry at a food shop. Everybody has to have food, and surely someone in her family would be going out to buy. He picked out a clean-looking fish market on St. George Street and forced himself to walk in the front door.

Inside, the proprietor eyed him from back of the counter. Rod fumbled in his pocket for the picture, drew it out and held it before the man.

"Do you know this girl?" he asked, his tongue stumbling over the words.

The fish seller wiped his hands on his apron. "Let me see her close, lad." He reached for the painting.

"Fine picture of Dolly James," he said absently, as if to himself. And to Rod, "Want me to give it to her, lad? She's just up the street a ways, at the bakery."

Rod's pulse jumped. "No, thanks," he mumbled, reaching for his prize. "I'll take it. No use making you leave your shop."

The man walked to the door with Rod. "There," he said, pointing down the street, "the James Bakery. T'ain't more'n half a block. You'll see the sign."

Rod started in that direction, excited and scared that he had at last found Dolly James. But he was relieved, too. The fear that she might live in one of the many big houses, with rugs on the floor and chairs so ornate he wouldn't dare sit in one, had worried him a good bit since coming to St. Augustine.

He saw the bakery when still several doors away. Its modest blue and white sign reassured him. But as he came abreast of the window, a shock tingled through him. For there, arranging a display of cream tarts, was the girl of the miniature.

Her eyes were just as blue as the painting, and her tilted nose was covered wth tiny freckles. She wore a white apron over a blue dress, and her light-brown hair, drawn back sharply from her face, fell in a cascade of wavy locks over her shoulders.

She looked so pleasant that he almost said hello, but remembered that she didn't yet know him.

Suddenly she vanished, and when he entered the bakery, she was taking crusty rolls from a long pan.

"Did you want bread?" she asked politely. And when Rod didn't answer, "It's just out of the oven. Or would you like some of these fresh rolls?"

"Neither, thanks," said Rod. He drew the painting from his pocket. "I found this," he blurted, "in the woods near Wahoo Swamp."

He was unprepared for the girl's quickly drawn breath as she reached for the picture. For an instant she looked at it, then bent her head so Rod couldn't see the tears. When they began to splash down her cheeks, she raised a corner of her apron and wiped them away. Rod thought he heard her say, "Oh, Papa!" very softly.

"I'm sorry, miss," said Rod unhappily.

At last she looked up. "Excuse me," she apologized. "Papa had this picture made a year ago last spring so he could carry it with him. He went out with the Florida volunteers."

She didn't need to tell Rod any more. Somewhere her father had fallen—perhaps in the very woods near Wahoo, where Rod had found the painting.

She touched the mangled place in the frame. "This broken place," she asked in a muffled tone, "was it this way when you found it?"

"I'm terribly sorry, miss," he said again. "It was perfect when I found it." He told her the story of the Indian's bullet.

Her face brightened. "You mean the picture kept you from being hurt?"

"Yes, miss. I owe you my deepest thanks."

She smiled then. "I'm glad you found my picture."

A fair-haired, energetic woman carrying a pan of fresh-baked bread entered the shop from the kitchen. She looked much like Dolly, only older. She bustled to wait on a customer and talked pleasantly about the weather while she wrapped bread and cream tarts. When the customer was gone, Dolly introduced Rod:

"Mama, this is Rod Wheeler. He's a scout with the army. He's been over on the Little Withlacoochee, fighting Indians. He brought me this!"

She fished the miniature from the depths of her apron pocket and handed it to her mother.

Mrs. James looked at the painting for a long time without speaking. At last she said, "We're glad to have this, son. They sent us his gun and personal papers. But we often wondered what happened to Dolly's picture."

"Yes, ma'am," said Rod, somewhat at a loss for words.

Dolly saw his discomfort and changed the subject. "Where do you live?"

"On a farm near Fort Brooke."

"I was raised on the St. Johns—my father used to have a farm, too!"

The words pleased Rod. Then they were both farm people. It was almost like going home and meeting old friends.

"Stay to lunch," invited Mrs. James, "and you and Dolly can get acquainted. It's almost noon, anyway."

Rod was taken by surprise. "Why, I . . ." he stammered, embarrassed, "I'm afraid I can't." He wanted to stay, but his old leather coat and homespun seemed out of place in this spotless bakery. And he wished he'd had his hair cut the way John Fox said.

"Stay!" urged Dolly. "We have cream tarts today, and they're the very best thing Mother bakes."

"I'm afraid . . ."

"Stuff and nonsense!" said Dolly briskly, "you can stay if you want to. Besides, you ought to let us pay you back for returning the miniature." She took down an empty pan and began putting cream tarts into it. "How many can you eat, Rod? Four or six?"

"Four," said Rod modestly.

Dolly and Rod ate in the James' living quarters above the bakery. He was surprised to find that the furniture wasn't much more elegant than in his own farm home, except for a shabby carved-mahogany sofa that took up one whole wall, and two family portraits in oils that looked down solemnly from above the fireplace. The dining table was made of pine, with benches along each side, and Dolly served the simple meal of bread and cold partridge on pewter plates, with pewter mugs of cool spring water to wash it down.

The tarts were more luxurious, for they were baked for

the wealthier families in the city. Rod was impressed with
their rich crusts and creamy centers, and in praising them
forgot his earlier shyness. Once the conversation was well
started he told Dolly about his life on the Hillsborough
farm and his service in the army, about his parents and his
brothers, Hugh and small David.

Dolly described her father's farm near Jacksonville and
related how she and her mother had tried to raise cotton
by themselves but had failed.

"A bakery's better for two women," the girl confided.
"People are nice to us here, and we're doing very well. And
there's lots of fun in town that you don't have in the
country."

Rod agreed, wondering what she meant.

"We have dances every week at the schoolhouse, and
some of us girls meet on Thursdays to learn sewing. I make
my own clothes now," she said proudly.

Impressed, Rod glanced at her dress, thinking it looked
just as good as the clothes his own ma sewed.

"I have a new pink one I'm going to wear to . . ." She
paused suddenly. "Rod—would you like to go to the dance
Saturday?"

Rod stiffened with apprehension. Here she was again,
urging him into something that was unfamiliar and slightly
appalling. He had never gone to a dance, never even considered going.

"Why, I . . ." he began searching painfully for a polite
way to refuse.

"We girls are taken by our parents, of course, or older people," Dolly hurried on. "But you could go over with me and I'd help you get acquainted."

"I've never . . ." he began again.

Dolly interrupted. "Don't say you can't dance, because it doesn't make any difference. We're all learning, and it won't matter if you do make mistakes. Come on, Rod, please go," she pleaded.

Refusing was just too hard. Rod didn't know the proper phrases, so he looked out the window, fidgeted and finally said, "All right."

The four days until the dance seemed endless. He worried about what to wear and how to act. The thought of dancing—especially with Dolly—filled him with misgivings, and he dared not make many preparations for fear of being "joshed" by John Fox.

He did buy a new pair of moccasins, thinking guiltily that his mother might not approve because she could make them so cheaply at home. After trying to wash his homespun shirt, he decided it still looked unfit, so he had it laundered and ironed to an elegant smoothness.

The evening of the dance, his hair slicked back with water and his face scrubbed clean as a brook stone, he went to the rooms above the bakery to call for Dolly. She was sitting on the shabby mahogany sofa, waiting for him. He drew a deep breath when he saw her, for she wore a pale-pink frock and her brown hair was in braids across her head. She looked alarmingly grown up and lovelier even than in the miniature. His homespuns, clean as they were, suddenly seemed unsuitable. He wished desperately that he were back in his tent, where the volunteers thought more about marksmanship than clothes.

"How nice you look," greeted Dolly, rising to meet him. "Do you like my new dress? I had to hurry to finish it this afternoon."

The friendly words relieved Rod. "It's mighty pretty."

Mrs. James called up the stairs from the bakery.

"I see the Johnsons' cart coming."

"We're to go with them," Dolly explained. "They're chaperones for the dance."

All the way to the schoolhouse, Rod was self-conscious, for he never had escorted a girl anywhere before. But when they got inside with the crowd and heard the fiddlers tuning up, his mood began to change. He would learn to dance, he vowed, if it took his last breath. And he'd dance well, just as he hunted and trapped.

Dolly introduced him to her friends: "This is Jane, this is Miranda, and Polly, with the yellow ribbons."

Mostly they were girls about Dolly's age who wore fullskirted dresses and had their hair hanging down their backs. They acknowledged the introduction but immediately began chattering among themselves, as if they couldn't think of any small talk to exchange with this strange young man.

The boys had congregated in another corner, and Rod felt he ought to join them, but the music struck up, everybody moved toward the center of the floor, and the caller bellowed, "All join hands . . ."

From that time until the first dance ended, leaving the dancers out of breath and laughing, Rod strove hard to do everything right. The steps weren't too intricate, he discovered, and he knew that before the evening was through he would be dancing just as well as the rest. He sought out Dolly, who had been on the other side of the room when the music ended.

"How'd you like it, Rod?" she asked, her eyes luminous.

"Fine," he replied honestly.

"You've danced before—I know it!"

He protested that he hadn't, but she didn't seem to believe him. To hide his too-obvious pleasure, he glanced around the room to where the boys and girls now were talking together.

"Who are those fellows in the swallowtails?" he asked, looking enviously at three or four boys who were dressed as he had wanted to be.

To his surprise, Dolly's small nose seemed to turn up as she replied, "Those are Tories, Rod—or rather the sons of Tories. You know St. Augustine's full of people who don't like the soldiers very well and sympathize only with the Indians. Of course, I guess if you were English, or felt allegiance to the crown, you naturally wouldn't like people who revolted and won their freedom, would you!"

"I guess not," replied Rod, warmed by her loyalty and glad that he was not inside one of those fine suits. Hart had been right, he reflected, when he said Dolly didn't like swallowtails.

"St. Augustine used to be English," Dolly reminded him, "and then lots of Tories came here from the States, just because they didn't want to join the Revolution. During the war, John Hancock and Samuel Adams were burned in the public square!"

"Burned?" echoed Rod. He didn't remember any such happening from his history books.

She laughed. "Not really. Just little figures of them. They call it burning them in effigy."

Rod relaxed and laughed with her, thinking how foolish he had been to try to refuse her invitation to the dance.

Dolly's friends, most of them not so well dressed as the Tories, welcomed Rod and took him at once into their circle. The boys looked up to him, for he was older than they and had been with the army. One of them, Jim Jeffers, insisted that Rod stop dancing and tell them about the battle of Wahoo Swamp. But Rod only smiled and whirled Dolly toward a new group that was forming for a quadrille.

Later he and Dolly drank orange punch and sampled the molasses cookies which Dolly had brought as her share of the evening's refreshments.

"Is it anywhere near ten o'clock, I wonder?" asked Rod when they had finished. Although he didn't have a watch and couldn't see the moon to gauge the hour, he was used to guessing time, and it seemed as if it might be nearly ten, the hour for the dance to end.

"Yes," sighed Dolly, "I guess so. I see Mrs. Johnson motioning to us now."

"Let's go then."

Together they rode in the Johnsons' cart down the dark streets of St. Augustine toward the bakery. Rod never would have guessed a week ago that this strange city, so awesome at first, would have accepted him as a part of it. But here he was, knowing people, going to dances, and even taking a girl home! It almost scared him.

Chapter 11

Slowly the Tide Turns

"Let the chiefs and warriors know that we have been deceived by them long enough and that we do not intend to be deceived again. Order the whole party directly to town. You have force sufficient to compel obedience and they must move instantly."

—Major General Thomas S. Jesup
in a letter to Brigadier General
J. M. Hernandez, Oct. 21, 1837

IN SEPTEMBER of 1837, King Philip, descendant of a royal Seminole line, was captured at a coastal camp below St. Augustine, along with other chiefs and their followers. He was brought to Fort Marion and confined within its twelve-foot-thick walls.

From inside his prison the chief sent frantic word begging his son, Coacoochee, to come to him.

While the messenger sought Coacoochee in forests to the south, the American general, Joseph M. Hernandez, waited quietly at his headquarters in St. Augustine. He hated Indians, for they had destroyed all his properties. Only by assuming leadership of the East Coast militia had he saved the settlements from further ravaging. But his dark eyes, indicative of his Spanish ancestry, were contented now, for he had captured a strong warrior-chief and could hope that Coacoochee, most savage fighter of them all, would come in.

The men at the camp were quiet, too, hiding their exultation as they saw the advantage swing farther to their side.

At their tent, Rod, Hart and John Fox were cleaning up. Ants had discovered some sweetmeats belonging to Fox, and one whole corner of the enclosed spot had to be cleaned out thoroughly. Rod was redigging the rain trench while Hart mended a hole in his blanket.

While they worked, they talked, discussing everything from war to the best way to cook venison. Rod had just remarked that Dolly told him she cooked venison basted with crab-apple jelly. He bit his lip the minute he had said it, wishing he had kept still.

"She does, does she?" commented Fox dryly. "Well, be careful, my boy. That's the way bridegrooms are made."

Rod's face reddened. "She isn't thinking about that," he protested. "She's learning to cook, that's all."

Hart chimed in, half teasing, half defending. "Let him alone, Fox, let him alone. If I could get as many cream tarts by visiting the bakery, I'd go there, too."

"You can get them, but not free," observed Fox, "and therein lies the difference."

"Quit!" exclaimed Rod indignantly. The teasing riled him, although he knew it was meant in a friendly spirit.

He changed the subject sharply. "When are they going to issue more rations?"

"Tomorrow," replied Fox blandly, as he looked for ants under his blanket roll. "But cream tarts or no cream tarts, she has the most fascinating blue eyes I've ever seen. Did you ever see such blue eyes, Hart?"

"Never," agreed Hart.

"Stop it!" roared Rod.

Both his friends burst into loud laughter, and Rod dug his shovel sharply into the rain trench.

"Hey, wait!" exclaimed Hart. "When it rains we'll have a lake there! Quit joshing him, Fox. He's had enough!"

A soldier hurried past, then another, running toward the Spanish house that served as headquarters. Rod looked in that direction. Everywhere men were hurrying toward the red-roofed building.

"Something's happened!" He dropped his shovel and without waiting for the others ran to where a crowd was gathering near the entrance to the structure.

As he stood, craning his neck but not seeing anything unusual, Fox and Hart caught up.

"Coacoochee's coming in!" the scout exclaimed. "Fellows, things surely are rolling our way!"

At that instant they spotted the young warrior, walking between two American soldiers toward the door of the fort. Coacoochee was slight and wiry, his face small-featured as the face of a girl. He walked with the grace of grasses swaying in the wind. Although he had the shy, wild look of a woods' creature, his black eyes burned darkly in his face, like the disillusioned eyes of an old man.

In one hand he carried a white plume, in the other his long rifle. Without looking to right or left, he marched straight to the doorway. One of the soldiers held it open and he entered.

"No surrender in sight, from the looks of him," observed John Fox. "He still hates us all. What's your bet, Hart?"

Hart frowned thoughtfully. "He looks a lot different from his father. But then King Philip was brokenhearted over his capture. Coacoochee is free—coming in under a feather of truce. He hasn't that sense of defeat."

Rod agreed with John Fox. Coacoochee had a stubborn, independent look, and unmistakable hatred in his eyes.

"Scout Whitley!" called someone from the door of the headquarters. "Come inside! We need you to interpret."

"Good-bye, fellows," said Hart. He turned and began pushing through the crowd.

"Irritating," remarked John Fox, "but we'll hear all about it later. Wonder how long he'll be gone?"

"Couple of hours, I suppose."

"That's about it. Let's finish the tent, sonny."

Rod overlooked the word "sonny" and went back to the tent, which he and Fox made clean and tidy. When they were through, Fox lighted a pipe and began to discourse on the broader aspects of the war, his favorite subject:

"If Secretary of War Poinsett could see this war as it

really is, the soldiers would be out of here in sixty days. Taking over a wilderness when nobody wants to settle there is ridiculous." He tamped tobacco into his pipe. "If the Indians could get a reservation in the south of the state, they'd be satisfied. The promises in the Treaty of Fort Moultrie would be honored at last, and we'd all go home and enjoy sitting at a table for breakfast. By the way," he added, "I'm getting some money on the post tomorrow and I'm going to put my knees under a table and have somebody serve me a good meal if I die indigent."

"Good idea," said Rod absently.

"You and Hart and I can get a real dinner at the Buck and Ball Coffee Shop on St. George Street. They do it up brown, the men say—roasts, stuffing, puddings—anything you like."

Rod didn't answer.

"Ever been to the Buck and Ball?"

"No. I—I think maybe I'd better drop out of the plans."

"Going to see Dolly?"

Rod crimsoned. "No."

"Then what's wrong with going to the coffee shop?"

Rod picked up a bit of coquina rock and threw it a long way. "I never ate in a coffee shop!" he blurted out finally. "I'd feel like a—never mind, I just don't like coffee shops."

John Fox started to laugh, but changed his mind and became deadly serious. "For your own good, Rod, you must come to the coffee shop. You might find yourself a landed gentleman some day, and wish to know the correct use of knife, fork and spoon." With hardly a change in expression, he crossed the line from serious to ridiculous. "The principle is extremely simple: one conveys food from plate to mouth, keeping the crumbs to a minimum. Again. And again." He demonstrated with an imaginary fork.

"Keep still!" exclaimed Rod.

"But," Fox ignored him and lifted a finger dramatically, "there is one quality of prime importance. A gentleman has self-confidence; an oaf has none. Therefore you must come to the coffee shop and acquire poise."

"Oh, all right," agreed Rod, feeling trapped.

Hart returned in less than an hour. He brought exciting news.

"Coacoochee is going to bring in all the Seminoles on the St. Johns River!" he told Rod and Fox, who were rigging some fishing lines while they waited.

"You mean both Coacoochee and the king have given up?" asked Fox, incredulous.

"Both of them!"

"Hooray!" Fox tossed his fish pole in the air and caught it as it fell groundward.

"You mean they're willing to abide by the treaties, the way General Jesup wants?" persisted Rod, still dubious.

"That's what Coacoochee said."

"It's hard to believe."

"It's mighty comfortable to believe," paraphrased Fox.

"C'mon," urged Hart, "let's walk along the wall." And as the others followed him, he went on, "There's more to it—and all good. Don't know when I've heard so much favorable war news."

"More!" echoed Rod. It seemed as if there couldn't be anything else.

"Yep. This is it. Osceola sent a white feather and a bead pipe by Coacoochee. His message was that 'the way is safe and white' for General Fernandez to come see him, and would it be the same if he came to see the general? Cohadjo sent the same word."

Rod said nothing. He was dazed with so much good fortune.

John Fox nodded decisively. "It's the big break, at last," he said. "The Indians can't get away with any of that desertion stuff again, and they know it. This time we'll get the cream of the tribes and ship them west."

The whole camp was on tenterhooks the next few weeks, while Coacoochee went out to deliver gifts from the general and take a message to Osceola and Cohadjo. He also was to round up King Philip's people and bring them in. A date in October had been set for Coacoochee's return, so that there would be no lag in the operations.

Promptly on the day set, the slight young warrior returned, and again was ushered in to see General Hernandez. He brought word that Osceola's band and Cohadjo's were at Fort Peyton, seven miles south of the city. They would await a conference.

"Fort Peyton!" exclaimed Rod, when he heard. "Think of it, only a few miles from here!" He wondered excitedly if he could go with the general. But word came soon that Hart was to go as interpreter. Rod had been assigned to guard duty at Fort Marion.

"Worse luck!" muttered John Fox when he heard that Rod would have to stand all day before the ancient moat. "Just when you could see Osceola without risking your neck, you have to tote a gun back and forth in front of that rock-pile!"

Rod, too, was irked, but he said nothing. Maybe John Fox would forget about the dinner. Guard duty was monotonous, but if it eased him out of a social crisis like eating at the coffee shop, he was willing to keep it up indefinitely.

"But we'll still be able to go to dinner," added Fox suddenly.

The elegance of the Buck and Ball was oppressive to Rod. There was spotless white linen on every table, pewter knives, forks and spoons, thin-lipped coffee cups and colored drinking glasses so fragile he was afraid to touch one of them.

Through air noisy with talk and heavy with tobacco smoke he glanced around at the other taper-lighted tables. The men sitting there were mostly dressed in fashionable long-tailed coats over frilled shirts and flowered waistcoats. But Rod was relieved to see that some diners wore homespun garments and leather moccasins, as if they had just come in from a hunting trip.

Rod and Fox had waited until the last minute for Hart,

hoping he would get home early from the conference with Osceola. Finally they had gone off, leaving him a note to join them if he arrived back at camp in time.

To Fox the coffee shop acted as a stimulant. He was in good spirits, smiling, telling Rod anecdotes of his youth and fingering the thin glassware as if it made him homesick.

"You know I was born to much better than this, Rod," he said once, as if in explanation.

Fox ordered for them both: Roast venison, duck, Yorkshire pudding and pumpkin pie. Rod had just taken up his fork when the door opened and Hart stepped inside. The scout was pale and tired. His eyes were gloomy.

He glanced around at the diners, found his friends, and at once came to their table.

"What happened?" asked John Fox, whose quick eyes had spotted signs of trouble.

Hart paused to order dinner from the waiter and did not speak until the man was out of earshot. "Plenty," he replied. "We violated a flag of truce today."

Fox laid down his fork, stared at the scout. "We? Who is we?"

"The United States Army."

There was a shocked silence.

"How?" asked Fox at last.

"Took Osceola and Cohadjo and all their followers. Dumped their white flag on the ground and later rolled it up and put it into somebody's saddlebag."

There was silence. Even Fox had no ready reply this time. Finally he said, "Tell us about it."

Hart leaned forward so he could speak softly without being overheard.

"We all thought we were going to a conference," he began, "but at the last minute orders were changed. We were told to seize the two leaders and all their bands."

"Whose idea was that?" asked John sharply. "Surely Hernandez . . ."

Hart broke in. "General Jesup, I'm sure. Hernandez wouldn't dare do such a thing on his own authority."

Rod thought back to the stern general who had dickered with the Indians at Fort Dade. "General Jesup has always thought the Indians were violating their treaties," he remarked.

"Yes," agreed Fox, "and now he's carried that idea to its logical conclusion—he's captured them, ignoring their white flag! It's fantastic! Go on, Hart."

The scout took a gulp of water. "Osceola and Cohadjo were all decked out in their ceremonial robes—scarlet turbans, black ostrich plumes, silver necklaces, the whole rigging. They thought they were coming to a parley of top leaders. General Hernandez and the officers were in full dress, too."

"The actors arrived in the wrong costumes," observed John Fox bitterly.

"They did," said Hart. "They'd rehearsed the wrong lines, too."

"What'd they say?"

"Not very much. They advanced behind a white flag. When they were close enough to talk, Osceola began a dignified palaver about friendship and provisions. General Hernandez shot some questions at him—read them from a paper."

"Questions?" Fox's eyebrows rose. "Questions sent by Jesup?"

"I guess so. He asked where the other chiefs were and why hadn't the Negroes surrendered? The same angry kind of talk that Jesup always uses to them."

"What happened then?" asked Rod tensely.

"Osceola stared. He looked sick. Then he turned to Cohadjo and said, 'I'm choked. You'll have to speak for me.'"

"He knew," said Fox.

"He must have guessed. Even before the soldiers were ordered to take him. I think he sensed the whole plot. He grabbed for his gun but somebody knocked him down with the butt of a musket. They put him in chains—Cohadjo, too. They're in Fort Marion now."

A wry smile twitched the corners of Fox's mouth. "We've broken the fighting code," he said flatly.

Hart nodded. "Busted it wide open."

They sat silently. There seemed to be nothing to say.

"Hush!" put in Rod. "What's that?"

From far off came the sound of shouting, then the

pounding of hoofs as three horses galloped past the coffee shop. The restaurant quieted as everyone listened.

"Osceola's taken!" came a shout.

A cheer went up from the diners. It was echoed outside in the streets, a jubilant sound. Chairs scraped back from tables, men grabbed their guns and left. As they crowded toward the door, someone from outside called, "Osceola's been taken! He's up at the fort! He's behind bars!"

Rod, Hart and John Fox sat stonily. They had heard the news first and now they watched the reaction of the others.

The diners who had remained called for tankards from which to drink toasts.

"Here's to peace!"

"Here's to General Hernandez!"

"Here's to the Territory of Florida!"

Cider and ale were downed and the mugs refilled. Two frontiersmen and an English gentleman locked arms and began singing a victory song.

But when word leaked out that a white flag had been violated, the celebrations quieted. Men congregated in knots and heatedly discussed whether it was right or wrong.

Hart had eaten a hasty dinner. Now he rose. "Let's get out," he urged, moving toward the door. Fox and Rod followed.

In the street they encountered a crazy, excited mob. People were cheering General Hernandez, calling Osceola a murderer. Others were parading, giddy with the spirit of carnival. Now and then someone bellowed something about a white flag, but these few were shouted down.

"It doesn't take much," observed John Fox sourly, "to please some very pious folks."

"They'll get around to thinking tomorrow," said Hart.

Rod looked at Fox. "Going to whittle another notch in the butt of your rifle?"

"Yep. A fine large one."

"What are you going to do with that gun when it's all hacked up?" the boy asked curiously. "It won't be a decent gun any more. What good will it do anybody?"

Fox cleared his throat importantly. "I'm going to give it to a museum," he answered, with more than his usual mock seriousness. "It's getting old-fashioned, and I hope to replace it with a breechloader. The notches will help me drive a better money bargain. You see, Rod," he added grimly, "most monuments remind us of something praiseworthy we have done. Mine will be different."

"Very different," agreed Hart, without smiling.

Chapter 12

The Stranger

"As I had informed the chiefs at Fort King that I would hold no communication with the Seminoles unless they should determine to emigrate; as I had permitted no Indian to come in for any other purpose but to remain; as they were all prisoners of war, or hostages who had violated their parole; as many of them had violated the truce entered into at Fort King by occupying the country east of the St. Johns, by allowing predatory parties to go to the frontier and by killing at least one white man; and as the white flag had been allowed for no other purpose than to enable them to communicate and come in without danger of attack from our parties, it became my duty to secure them, on being satisfied of the fact that they intended to return to their fastnesses. I accordingly required General Hernandez to seize them and take them to St. Augustine; but notwithstanding their character as prisoners and hostages who had violated their parole, and who according to the laws of war as recognized by civilized nations had forfeited their lives, I directed that they should be treated with every kindness and have every accommodation consistent with their security."

—Major General Thomas S. Jesup
in an official report

THE SUN had relaxed its penetrating warmth and was merely a sparkle on the thick coquina walls of Fort Marion. Rod felt the cool of evening stealing across the bay and figured it would be another hour before he could quit his guard duty.

He was tired of pacing beside the sluggish water of the prison moat and disliked the weight and coldness of the fort itself, so reminiscent of Spanish power. For it was built, he had been told, to protect Spain's "treasure fleet," plying between Mexico, Peru and the mother country, with gold looted from ancient civilizations.

In spite of his aversion, Rod realized that assignment to this duty was an honor. For now the old dungeon held its most illustrious prisoners of the entire Seminole War. Osceola—greatest Indian leader of the Territory—was there, and Chief Cohadjo. King Philip had been joined by his son, Coacoochee, who had found that his white feather was no protection after all.

Rod had seen the captives in the half dusk of their solid-rock cell, which was aired and lighted only by a narrow window slit high above the floor. They were a soul-sick lot. The proud Osceola seemed to have set his face toward death. He took no interest in those around him but stared stonily ahead, eating his food absently, obeying his guards, and sometimes pacing the floor for hours at a time.

Coacoochee had reacted differently. Astonished at the fate of his white feather, his black eyes reflected more deep and terrible angers than before. Almost at once he became ill and requested certain roots from the forest. But their medicine only melted away his remaining flesh, until the bones showed starkly beneath his skin.

King Philip, still a sturdy warrior at sixty, said little. Only Cohadjo expected release. Whining, he reminded his guards that he had tried to cooperate with the white general and should be considered his friend.

The truce violation—first such blot on the official record of the army in Florida—stirred public emotion everywhere. Although jubilance had marked the early report that Osceola and Cohadjo were in chains, second thought made many question the method. Groups in both South and North—even the soldiers themselves—resented the desecration of the white flag, which over the years had acquired almost a sanctity among nations. Newspapers began to publish editorials attacking General Jesup, and in taverns and coffee shops the capture was discussed with more and more heat until it became a sore point.

Soon Osceola and Cohadjo, in spite of the trick that had been played on them, sent word from their cells that they wanted to call in their people. They would surrender and wished the others to go also. They had had enough.

Immediately General Jesup sent a young chief and two warriors to round up the bands. Those who were willing to come in were told to meet the general at Fort Mellon on Lake Monroe, or General Hernandez at New Smyrna.

Again the settlers began to hope for peace. But this time they stayed near the forts and waited, afraid to venture back to their farms until the enemy's promises had been fulfilled.

Word came that Micanopy had appeared at Fort Mellon with eighty warriors. They camped near the fort, their number increasing daily. The news was cheering. In time, perhaps, most of the Indians who had deserted at Fort Brooke would again come in.

But just when it seemed that a great migration would take place without resort to arms, the Seminoles were surrounded, bound and sent to St. Augustine.

General Jesup's second truce violation was attended by more public indignation, and John Fox unobtrusively enlarged the truce violation notch he had put in his "museum gun."

Rod watched the sun drop lower, projecting the great shadow of the fort onto the beach, then over the water. The cirrus clouds above the bay glowed pink and mingled their reflections with the gray-blue of tugging currents. It was nearly time to quit—less than an hour—and Rod wondered idly what Hart and John Fox planned to do that evening.

Absently he noted a rickety wagon jouncing between the thick coquina pillars of the city gate. It was drawn by a bony old horse and held a load of junk. From where Rod stood, he could see bundles of hides, a broken wagon wheel and a litter of smaller objects which piqued his curiosity.

To his surprise, the wagon came up the hill toward the fort and stopped not far from the moat. Its driver alighted slowly. He was an odd-looking fellow with short black ringlets and a curly beard that billowed across his chest. He reached behind the wagon seat and drew up a gunny sack, which he slung over his shoulder as he turned toward the prison.

Rod wondered why he was bringing his load here. If he wanted to sell, the plaza was swarming with people, both soldiers and townsfolk.

As the fellow drew near, Rod saw that his nose was curiously misshapen, gnarled and twisted like a piece of driftwood.

In accordance with his orders, Rod raised his gun and said, "Halt!"

The man stopped. He seemed to look at Rod for the first time. His eyelids drooped and he spoke in a high nasal voice.

"I bring root for Coacoochee."

"Roots?" echoed Rod, puzzled.

"I bring root for Coacoochee," the fellow repeated. "He is sick."

"Yes," replied Rod slowly, staring at the face with its weird nose. He could never have seen this man before, he told himself, for no one ever would forget that face. Yet there was something that nudged a memory.

"I take root in," said the man, starting past Rod with the sack.

Rod stepped back and jabbed his bayonet threateningly. Although he had heard about the roots which Coacoochee used for medicine, he had no orders to let anyone inside the fort. "Sorry," he said crisply, "I have no orders to admit you."

"I bring root for Coacoochee," the man insisted sharply. He tapped the sack with his forefinger. "Root!"

"Sorry," repeated Rod. "I can't let you go in without orders from headquarters."

To his amazement the man began to fumble in his pocket and at last drew forth a dirty, crumpled slip that said, "Admit to the fort with roots for Coacoochee." It was signed by General Jesup himself.

The signature looked authentic to Rod. Then he glanced at the date. The slip was two weeks old.

"Sorry," he said again. "This was written two weeks ago. I'll have to have one dated today."

The man jerked the paper out of Rod's hand, stuck it back into his shirt and turned angrily away. His gesture said plainly that he thought little of the young sentry. Rod watched him, puzzled, as he strode back to his rickety wagon, tossed the bag of roots into the midst of the junk, and drove off.

An hour or so later, when Rod was off duty, he happened to be walking outside the city wall and again saw the wagon. This time it was standing back in the woods and its owner was just coming through the city gate. He no longer carried the bundle, and Rod did not see it in the wagon.

Funny, the boy thought. The other sentry must have let him deliver the roots. Or else he had gone to General Jesup and received a new pass.

The young scout mulled over the incident as he walked along the shore, watching again the silvery struggle of the water around Anastasia Island. He had never known any man with such a nose, and only a few with such thick, curly beards. Beyond that, the root vendor was like lots of other undistinguished frontiersmen in his greasy hunting shirt and wrinkled leggings.

Why had Rod felt that twinge of recognition? He didn't know. Must be, he decided, the man looked like one of the soldiers. Or perhaps he had been a volunteer whose term had run out.

It was nearly midnight when Rod ducked into the tent and crawled between his blankets. He had eaten supper with Dolly and her mother and on his way home had lingered near the slave market, thinking of the days when black men had been brought here in chains from Africa to be auctioned off to the highest bidder.

Because it was late, he fell at once into a deep sleep.

At dawn he wakened, bathed in sweat and rigid with fear. In his mind was an image of the man he had seen the afternoon before. And now he remembered.

Except for the thick beard, short hair, and the strange nose, the fellow was Zade Galda!

The boy's reason resisted. Galda was dead. Shakochee had shot him. The fishermen had buried him on the mainland across from Cockroach Key. He couldn't be here in St. Augustine. Even if the beard could be explained, and the crippled nose, Galda was dead and could not be driving a cartful of junk around the city.

But his instinct told him it was so. Galda was here. He had disguised himself by cutting his long hair and growing a beard. The nose was harder to explain. But it could have been caused by a break, or a wound. And as the thought of a wound came to Rod's mind, his heart jumped. For he remembered Shakochee's rifle ball and the ribbon of red that had stained the surf of Tampa Bay.

Yes, the man was Zade Galda, Rod decided, no matter what the fishermen had said about burying him. He looked different, and he had discarded the hunting shirt with the bullet hole. But he was the same man, and up to no good, probably.

Rod remembered the roots in the gunny sack. Had Galda wanted to poison the Indian chief? That seemed unlikely, for Galda himself was a fugitive from the whites and would be more apt to help the Seminole prisoner. But what could be the explanation? Rod didn't know.

Of one thing he was sure. Whatever Zade Galda was doing was to benefit himself.

Chapter 13

Return to the Forest

"It was the first time in Florida that a flag of truce was ignored, under orders, by an officer of the U. S. Army —but not the last."

—Marjory Stoneman Douglas
in *The Everglades: River of Grass*

ALTHOUGH IT was well past midnight, the moon was still below the horizon, and darkness covered the bay with its chill, ocean-damp cloak. From where Zade Galda sat his pony in a sea-grape thicket outside the city gate, stars pierced the sky with the brilliance of meteors. Only one other light eclipsed them, the glow from a sentry's fire on the other side of the wall near the entrance to Fort Marion. Now that night had come, the guards had heaped it high and its flames sent a red-throated column of smoke into the night sky.

Galda shoved his curly black beard inside the neck of his hunting shirt and fretted at the slowness of time. His pony was restless, switching its tail, and stepping this way and that as mosquitoes bit at its flanks. Some of its nervousness passed to the extra mount whose rein Galda held. He cursed them both softly every time they agitated the sea-grape trees.

He was risking his neck, a job for which he had no zest, although the reward would be large. Lured on by the silver box, he had probed further and had gathered together half a dozen accounts of a treasure ship wrecked on the Keys and looted over the years by the Indians. Nothing was left, now that he had the silver box, but a small golden idol.

Many men had tried to own it, the story went, but one had died of fever, another had been murdered, and a third drowned. Now the golden god lay abandoned on a creek bank.

Zade chuckled. The farther away the Indians stayed from the god, the better. That much gold would be worth a fortune. He could get out of Florida Territory and the peddler's business forever. He could shave off this monstrous beard and maybe have a doctor straighten his ugly nose.

In Charleston or Savannah he could live as a respected man of property. Maybe he would be fantastically rich some day, for he had heard that it takes money to make money.

He glanced up at Jupiter sinking toward the treetops and thought that it must be nearly time for the escape. The star must even now be glittering through the high window slit of Coacoochee's cell in the fort.

Although he strained his eyes in the direction of the

fort wall, he could see little through the darkness and mist. There was nothing to do but wait. He had delivered a rope concealed among the roots, and the rest was up to Coacoochee.

A cold wind moved the sea-grape leaves, and from a fishing boat crossing the bay came the eerie wail of a conch-shell horn. At the noise, Zade's pony whinnied softly. The man cursed again and pulled harshly at the rein. His eyes flicked to the gate, afraid it would open and soldiers would come pouring out. But the wind was in the wrong direction and the solid stone of the gate did not move.

His thoughts turned angrily to Rod Wheeler and their meeting the previous afternoon. He had been careless in walking right up to the boy, but felt pride at the way he had fooled the young scout with his twanging voice and black beard. If only he had been alone with Rod, he might have settled the score then and there. For it would take a lot to make up for the deformed nose that Shakochee's bullet had given him and the prison sentence Rod had hung around his neck. It was Rod's fault, too, that he had fallen into the hands of those blackguardly fishermen, who had forced him to ransom himself.

He had one comforting thought from the past—his silver chest was safe. He had taken it to St. Augustine for storage and had done what he considered a very clever job of disguising it so that no one would suspect its value.

He glanced again toward the window slit of the fort,

and his muscles tensed. Something was moving there. Soundless, almost impossible to see against the prison's lichen-spotted walls, it nevertheless told Zade that the escape had begun.

The fort wall disappeared behind a veil of mist, and Zade could see nothing. He wondered if he had imagined that slight movement. Or, and his hopes dropped at the thought, perhaps Coacoochee could not force his body between the bars. Thin as he had made himself by taking the root medicine, he might still fail to slip through the window chink.

Above the wall, Galda could see the bayonets of two guards beside the fire, as if they had stopped to talk or light their pipes from an ember.

Ten minutes passed. He began to fidget. Something had to happen quickly. Soon the sky would brighten and the sun would begin its climb out of the ocean. The rope would be found or the plan in some way discovered. He would lose his reward, maybe his life. For even if he evaded the sentries, the Indians might think he had betrayed them and seek him out for punishment.

A faint brushing of leaves sounded just ahead. And again, closer. Zade stiffened, held his heels against the pony's sides, ready to ride.

There was silence. From just ahead came the soft mewing of a gull. Jubilant, Zade returned the signal.

A slender shadow emerged from the trees. Even in the darkness Zade could see the moat water dripping from

Coacoochee's clothes. The Indian did not speak but took the rein held out to him and leaped onto the extra pony. Galda led the way, turning his mount inland, along a trail which would take them around the city and to the south.

As his pony swung into a gallop and the night air bit his face with its sharp mist, Zade laughed with soundless exultation. He had succeeded. All his plans would be fulfilled. For the Seminoles could not refuse him what they had promised, now that their young prince was free.

Almost as important as his wish for reward was the sweet taste of his revenge. Coacoochee would ride south and call the remaining tribes to arms. The war would go on. The United States Army would have to fight again. He had paid them for putting him in prison.

For hours the two riders kept on, guided by the dim light of the new-risen moon and later by the unfolding day. Now and then they halted to breathe the horses, or to drink from a creek or spring.

At the last stop, Coacoochee spoke. "You go," he said gruffly, "I ride alone."

Zade was taken aback. "I am Zade Galda," he explained. "The one who brought you the rope."

Coacoochee stared. "I have seen you before. The nose is different, but the eyes I know—and there was a bullet hole in the shirt."

Self-consciously Zade put his hand to his shoulder, although he long ago had discarded the shirt with the bullet hole. "The Indian shot first," he protested. "It was not I who tried to kill. He was to blame."

He paused but Coacoochee still looked at him fixedly.

"The Indian thought I was his enemy," Zade hurried on, "but I was not. I am the Seminoles' friend. I have given you gunpowder and guns. The white army put me in prison because I was the Indians' friend."

"You have been your own friend first," replied Coacoochee.

Panic made Zade's voice a pitch higher. "I freed you. I brought the rope. I . . ."

Coacoochee cut him short. "What have my friends promised you?"

Zade was slow to answer. This antagonism was not what he had expected. He had thought Coacoochee would be anxious to reward him for a dangerous job. He wondered if perhaps he might say the wrong thing now and lose forever what he wanted so much.

"I have been promised the golden god," he spoke at last.

An expression of fear flitted across the Indian's face. "The golden god?" he whispered.

"Si," answered Galda, reassured. He hastened to tell about the bargain. "They said they will take me south and toward the setting sun, where lies the god. He is like a little man, they tell me, and has more than two arms. You know the one?"

Coacoochee nodded. His face was dark, and Zade could not see its expression clearly.

"You will see that they take me?"

The Indian hesitated. "Our people do not lie. But no warrior will touch the yellow god."

"Then take me to him," urged the Spaniard.

Coacoochee stared long at the man. Finally he nodded. "It is good that you take the god from its hiding place. With your own hand you must raise it up and carry it away."

Zade was pleased. That was what he wanted, complete possession of the little golden image. It was lucky that the Indians were afraid of it. He wondered what had scared them so they didn't even dare touch it.

It was late afternoon when he stood at the edge of a dark creek and stared excitedly at the far side of it. There a shiny object rose some four inches above the water. It was not unlike the stumpy branch of a small tree, except that it was shaped like a human arm and glistened dull yellow.

He peered furtively back through the bay trees just to be sure no living eyes could see him claim the idol. His Indian guide had disappeared miles back and there was no sign of him now. There was nothing near the creek, either, but a flock of white egrets along the bend.

Although his head pounded with excitement, he moved slowly. He laid down his gun, took off his moccasins, and waded cautiously into the water, scarcely feeling its coolness against his bare feet, or the softness of the miry bottom. The stream was deep. It came to his knees, then his waist, and in the middle, where the current was strongest, he had to swim a few strokes before striking bottom again. A good thing the golden god had fallen so near the edge, Zade thought. In the deep part of the channel it would have vanished forever, tumbling downstream with the current and finally being drifted over with silt.

He was lucky, lucky.

He could almost touch the golden arm. His wet hands reached for it, grasped it, drew the strange object from its muddy bed. His lips laughing uncertainly, eyes swimming with excitement, he stood looking at his treasure.

The small idol—for, as the Indians had said, it was a god from some far land—gazed back at him with muddied, enigmatic eyes.

"I do not know if you be man or lady," Zade addressed the metallic creature, "but it is true you have too many arms. What you do with all those arms? Fight, maybe?"

He wiped the water and mud from the idol and smiled at its heightened gleam. "Ah, you very shiny," he murmured, "I wish I need not sell you."

He waded back across the creek, again swimming a stroke or two with the god in one hand, and splashed through the shallows. With a single big step he scaled the low embankment.

For an instant he paused in the shielding bay thicket, wondering where he should hide the golden creature. It was larger than he had expected, and its outflung arms made it difficult for him to conceal it on his person. A leather knapsack or bag would be needed, he thought, when he got back to the settlements. Meantime he would stuff it inside his hunting shirt.

Still shaky with emotion, he tucked the idol in the crook of his arm and began untying the thongs that closed the shirt. As he stood there, barefoot, he heard a faint sound that struck through him harshly. Again it came—a low, dry rattle.

He leaped backward, putting all his strength into the effort, for he knew it might mean the difference between life and death. His feet came down on the slope and he fell, jarring the golden god out of his grasp. It went somersaulting down the bank and plunged into the dark water.

The snake, lashing out like a thick rope, fell short of its mark. Zade scrambled hastily to his feet, swung his rifle in a wide arc and broke the reptile's back.

He did not wait to see its final writhings but was down the creek bank, eyes searching wildly for the golden god. It was nowhere in sight. The surface of the water was brushed with wind ruffles and the placid green of lily pads. There was no glint of gold anywhere.

He dropped to his knees and groped in the shallows, feeling desperately sick and bereft. When he did not find the god, he waded again into the water, sliding his hands along the mucky bottom, going deeper and deeper until

he came to the center of the stream. There he dived for
an hour without grasping anything but handfuls of mud
and eelgrass.

Only then did he give up, crying openly and without
shame, as he had when he was a small boy.

Chapter 14

The Search

"But for this untoward event (Coacoochee's escape) the war would certainly have terminated at this juncture, instead of being renewed and prolonged, as it afterwards was, through several eventful and disastrous years."

—John T. Sprague
in *The Florida War*

ROD SAT up. It was nearly morning and a gray light showed beneath the rolled-up sides of the tent.

"Hart!" he called. "John!"

Both roused quickly. "What's wrong?" asked Hart. Fox grabbed for his gun and looked wildly around, his hair tousled.

"I figured out something," said Rod, still sick from that moment of recognition.

"Figured out something!" snorted Fox. "The square root of X, maybe?"

He was putting back his gun when Rod hurriedly continued: "Zade Galda's alive! He's here in St. Augustine. I saw him yesterday."

"Well, why didn't you tell us yesterday?" snapped Fox.

"Wait a minute," cautioned Hart. "Rod, what is this? We don't quite understand."

Rod was pulling on his clothes, tugging at them in irrational haste. "I saw Zade Galda yesterday," he repeated impatiently, "but I didn't recognize him. Just now I woke up and knew who he was. Quick, let's go!"

"Where'll we go?" drawled Hart. His deliberate manner was maddening to the excited Rod.

"To General Hernandez!"

"He isn't up yet."

"Well, then, let's find Galda—the three of us!"

"If you aren't a lunatic I never saw one!" exclaimed Fox, disgruntled at Rod's interruption of his rest. "Either go back to sleep or get out of here so we can snooze the few minutes that are left."

"But I saw him at the fort!" Rod continued worriedly. He told about the sackful of roots and the man's determination to take them to Coacoochee. "I think he finally got in, or left the roots. He's up to something!"

Hart, too, was getting on his clothes. "How come you didn't know him?" he asked curiously. "You've seen him often enough. How come he could talk to you without being recognized?"

"The fishermen said he was dead," Rod explained. "Besides, he's grown a beard. And something's happened to his nose—it's all twisted."

"I see," mused Hart.

Rod straightened up from tying his moccasins. "Ready?"

"Be with you in a minute."

Fox had lain down again, drawn up his blanket, and was already snoring gently. Hart held his finger to his lips. "Let him have his beauty sleep."

Rod chuckled. "He needs it."

Together the two of them left the tent and went toward General Hernandez' headquarters facing the plaza.

"Look," exclaimed Hart, as the general's aide, fully dressed and carrying his rifle, ran out the front door. "Something's happened."

They watched as the man sprang onto his horse and spurred it along the south trail.

"Think they're after Galda?"

"I doubt it."

The door of the old Spanish house was open and there was considerable activity inside.

"What's going on?" Hart asked a soldier who was coming out.

The fellow hurried past with hardly a glance. "Coacoochee's escaped."

"Coacoochee!" repeated Hart, dazed at the news.

Rod looked at his friend in stunned silence. It raced through his head that such an occurrence might mean disaster to the Territory. Coacoocheee was the fiercest warrior among the tribes. He had been chained and imprisoned. In anger he had broken free.

"What'll he do? Go to war again?"

Hart nodded. "I'm afraid so."

He turned back toward the camp. "Might as well forget Galda for a while. General Hernandez won't be interested now."

"Unless Galda had something to do with the escape," put in Rod.

The older scout paused and looked fixedly at Rod. "He might have, at that," he said slowly.

Rod's mind was leaping ahead. "Those roots—what could they . . . ?"

"A knife or a rope, maybe a file."

"Could have been hidden in them, easy," agreed Rod.

"We'd better report."

Together the two scouts turned back to General Hernandez' quarters. Inside they found the general sitting at his desk, gulping a cup of coffee while he jotted notes on a piece of foolscap. His dark hair had been plastered across his head with a hasty dash of water, and there were pouchy circles under his eyes. Their harried black depths seemed to say that he had been made to violate a flag of truce and that nothing good had come of it after all.

"Yes, men?"

"You tell it, Rod," urged Hart.

So Rod told of his encounter with Zade Galda outside Fort Marion and of his conversation with the man. Briefly he explained his former meetings with the trader.

The general listened intently. "A gunny sack full of roots," he repeated. "It could have been the rope. We figure Coacoochee had a rope to get down from the window." His manner grew brisk. "Where does Galda stay?"

"We don't know, sir."

"We'll send a search party out."

"Yes, sir."

They were dismissed. Outside the building Rod tugged at Hart's sleeve. "Wait—I want to say something."

The scout paused. "What?"

Rod hesitated. He wondered what his friend would think of his idea. It was unorthodox, but he burned to put it into action.

He spoke softly so no one could overhear. "That search party will never find Galda. What do you say we hunt for him ourselves?"

Hart didn't act surprised. He thought for a minute. "Zade's a bad one. But I don't think we can hunt for him unless the general orders us to. We're with the army and at his command."

"But we're not doing anything now. He won't know we're gone!"

Hart shook his head. "He might want some interpreting done. It would look mighty bad if we'd run off."

"Even for a couple of hours?"

"Nope. Sorry."

They walked back toward their tent. Rod tried to accept the situation, but an uneasiness boiled inside him. The search party would go looking for a man with a black beard. They'd hunt for half a day and probably come back with the wrong person. Then nothing more would be done. Rod himself wanted to search, to see that every clue was followed to its end. He had plenty of liberty— more than the other men—and he didn't believe the general would care a bit what he did with it.

John Fox was dressed and in a better mood. He had started a fire and brewed coffee. When they told him about Coacoochee's escape, he offered a single caustic comment as he blew a phantom kiss into the air. "Peace, good-bye again."

Rod was quiet during breakfast, but his thoughts would not turn away from Galda. When the morning meal was over and dishes had been scrubbed, he left the tent and hurried toward St. George Street. Maybe Dolly had heard of the Spaniard. Surely no one with a black beard and such a weird nose could escape the notice of everyone in St. Augustine.

Dolly was helping her mother in the kitchen behind the bakery. When Rod asked her about Galda, she stared at him, wide-eyed, across a panful of bread.

"Yes—I saw a man like that!"

"Where?" asked her mother quickly as if she thought Dolly must be mistaken.

"Here, Mother, in the shop. He came in to buy rolls. Lots of times. He's so ugly I couldn't forget him. His nose is badly broken or something."

"That was Galda!" exclaimed Rod excitedly. "When was he here?"

Dolly's face lost its glow. "Not for a long time, Rod. At least two or three weeks."

"Oh." Rod was disappointed. But he kept on with his questions: "Did you ever see him around town? Do you know where he lived?"

Dolly shook her head. "No, I'm afraid not."

"You can't remember anything else about him?"

"No."

"I'll go up and down the street. Maybe somebody else remembers him."

Rod turned to go, but before he reached the door, Dolly called him back. "Rod—I remember—he tried to sell me some blue ribbon once. I wouldn't buy it and he said he had some more with flowers in it." Her voice rose, "And I remember he said he was a trader!"

"That's right," agreed Rod, not too enthusiastic over this news. "I knew that. He drove an old wagon with a broken-down horse. But where . . ."

"I wouldn't worry any more about Mr. Galda," put in Dolly's mother decisively, her hands busy tucking a last loaf of bread onto the bread peel. "He'll hang himself eventually, with his misdeeds."

"But he hates Rod," protested Dolly. "He might harm him! And besides, the army wants Galda. He's an escaped prisoner."

"I think hunting escaped prisoners just isn't your job, Dolly," Mrs. James reproved her daughter.

"Yes, Mother," said Dolly meekly.

"Give me a hand with this bread, Rod," said Mrs. James, as she opened the oven door. "Dolly, you can make the tart shells while these loaves are baking. I think I hear a customer in the shop."

She went to the front of the bakery, leaving Rod and Dolly alone. Rod started to say good-bye, thinking he would look farther for Zade. But Dolly held her finger to her lips and motioned him to wait.

"Rod, I have an idea," she whispered, her voice taut. "There's an old horse and wagon been standing a ways out the Jacksonville road. I saw it last Friday when Mary Smythe and I rode up there to gather persimmons. It's near a little log cabin. Do you think it could be his?"

"You mean," asked Rod, only mildly interested, "that you think the wagon might be Zade Galda's?"

"It might be," she said solemnly. "It sounds like his. And if he's a trader, he'd have to have a place to keep his things besides that wagon."

Rod shook his head. "Most of the peddlers get along with a wagon. Some of them just carry a sack."

"But he could have a little house," insisted Dolly, deftly pinching flour and lard together for the tarts. "He could, you know, Rod."

"He could," agreed Rod. And because he had no other

clue, he added, "It's worth looking into. Along the north road, you say?"

"Let me take you there," begged Dolly, her eyes as shiny as ripe huckleberries. "I'll be through with the tart shells in less than an hour. And Mother promised I could have a day off this week. Please wait for me."

Rod promised just because she was so anxious. And to keep his Galda hunt from bogging down, he decided to walk through town, asking other shopkeepers if they remembered the Spaniard.

Although he went up and down the streets, nobody else seemed to remember the trader. The proprietor of the fish market said at first he had seen him, then wondered if he was imagining the whole thing, and at last said to find somebody else whose memory was better.

Discouraged, Rod returned to the bakery. The tarts were done and their tempting smell pervaded the kitchen. Dolly was waiting for him. She wore her "berrying" clothes, which were scratched with thorns. Near the door of the kitchen she had piled several buckets.

"We won't have time for a lot of persimmon hunting," Rod objected. "I've got to be back at camp before three o'clock. I stand late guard at the fort."

Dolly smiled eagerly. "It's not the persimmons I'm thinking about," she explained. "We have to appear to be doing something, you know. It isn't polite to peek into people's houses just out of curiosity."

"You're right," Rod admitted.

"Now, if you'll just help me carry out the buckets," she urged, "and hitch up old Maude to the wagon, we'll be out of here in a jiffy. Of course," she added apologetically, "I will have to bring back just a few persimmons—Mother's counting on them for bread, and we can always trade them to people who want to make beer."

Rod couldn't help but give back her smile. She was bound to hunt for Zade Galda, but she was going to have her persimmons, too. He guessed he'd have to humor her.

The broad trail leading north of the city was empty of people. In a short distance it led away from the ocean and plunged into stretches of thickly grown oak hammock or pine flats. Their cart passed two cabins, both deserted.

"The Parkers and the Andersons have moved into St. Augustine," Dolly explained. "There's one more farm, the McLeods', a mile beyond the cabin I told you about. The Indians tried to burn the McLeod house and nobody's lived there for a while. But just beyond it there's a wonderful place to gather persimmons."

"How many bucketfuls do you usually get?" Rod asked curiously.

"As many as I can," replied Dolly. "Two or three go a long way."

"And do you come way out here by yourself?"

Dolly looked shocked. "Never alone—Mother wouldn't allow it. Mary Smythe and I do, though. We aren't afraid."

Rod saw she meant it, and he admired her courage.

Maybe she wasn't the fragile little creature he had thought her when he found the small painting. He stole a glance at her resolute profile and decided she might even do her share of Indian fighting if she were a settler's daughter.

"There it is!" she said abruptly, as they rounded a curve and saw a palmetto-thatched log cabin ahead of them. "But the wagon's gone! There's only a saddled pony."

Rod was disappointed. "There must be lots of wagons that look like Zade Galda's."

"Yes," Dolly admitted weakly, "I suppose there are. "Please, Rod, don't be angry if he isn't here."

Rod tried to hide his chagrin. Just now, when he needed to be tracking down Galda, she had brought him way out here in the country on a wild goose chase! But he knew she meant well, had been trying to help.

"Never mind," he said gently, "it would be almost too much good luck to find him on the first try."

As they came closer to the cabin, Rod saw that it was set well off the trail in a little clearing. The front door was closed and no smoke came from the chimney. But that saddled pony outside said plainly that someone was inside.

"What shall we do?" asked Dolly. "Knock on the door and ask for a drink of water?"

"If Zade Galda saw me standing at his front door, he'd yank out his knife and I wouldn't ever again need a drink of water," Rod objected.

Dolly looked scared. "Then let's pick persimmons and watch. Maybe he'll come outside."

"There aren't any persimmon trees around here."

After a look along the trail, Dolly agreed. "There really isn't anything that we could be gathering," she commented bleakly. "The persimmons are farther on."

"Then let's drive past."

"That would be easiest," Dolly admitted, "but we wouldn't find out anything."

Rod had a plan. "Let's drive past, leave the cart, and sneak back here," he suggested. "We could watch the cabin from that thick patch of woods to the left."

"I hate to leave old Maude," Dolly was saying. "Mother wouldn't . . ."

She broke off in the middle of her sentence. "Rod, look!"

A man had come out of the dwelling and was walking toward the pony. He was a Spaniard—perhaps part Indian—and tall and husky. From the wagon they caught a glimpse of his face. His rather large nose was long and straight. He was not Zade Galda.

Rod felt a keen pang. Dolly's hunch had really been a fizzle. This proved it. The wagon she saw could easily have belonged to someone else. Even if it was Zade Galda's it might have been left there while the trader was selling to someone in this cabin.

Wordlessly, the two young people watched the tall man climb into the saddle without once looking in their direction, rowel his horse, and ride north. The fast pace of his mount soon took him out of sight among the trees.

"Guess we'd better find a few persimmons and then go home," said Rod glumly.

"Well, I'm not ready to give up," announced Dolly, her voice edged with annoyance. "I'm going to see the inside of that cabin."

Rod looked at her, surprised. "How?"

"I'm going to knock at the door and ask if the McLeods live here."

"But nobody's home," objected Rod. "The fellow that lives there just rode away."

"Maybe he has a wife," countered Dolly, "or a partner. I'm going to knock and see."

"All right," agreed Rod. It wouldn't hurt, he thought, to indulge her a little. The trip had been a time-waster and she was embarrassed. Best to let her do as she asked. Maybe she wouldn't feel so bad.

He started to turn the horse into the clearing, but she stopped him. "Wait here. I'll walk to the house."

Rod obediently reined the horse. "Why?"

"Well, if Zade Galda should be there . . ."

Rod tried to conceal his smile. It amused him to see what a bulldog determination Dolly had. Here she was, still thinking that Zade Galda might be in that cabin.

The cart came to a stop, and Dolly climbed out, taking care not to catch her full skirt. Although she appeared calm, there were spots of red in her cheeks. She walked resolutely across the clearing and Rod saw her raise one hand and knock briskly at the door.

Nothing happened and she knocked again. She stood there a long time, but nobody came to answer. Again she knocked.

Why doesn't she come back? Rod thought impatiently. Nobody's home but she hates to admit that her scheme is no good.

To his surprise he saw the door suddenly swing inward. He heard no one speak, but Dolly stepped into the cabin, out of sight.

The roots of his hair prickled. Who had opened that door? What had happened to Dolly? He was scared.

But before he could think what to do, Dolly appeared at the door and beckoned him. It was a hasty gesture. Again she vanished inside.

Rod looped the reins around the whipsocket and leaped off the cart. He strode across the clearing and got to the cabin in a few seconds. The door still was standing open and he hurried through it.

There was Dolly in the center of the single room. Although no one else was present, the place certainly wasn't empty. It was piled high with everything under the sun, old saddles, bits of harness, dilapidated kegs, pieces of cloth, a gray blanket with a large burned hole in it—even a pile of the commonest seashells seemed to say that the owner of this place never discarded a thing.

"Look, Rod!" Dolly exclaimed. "Did you ever see such a spot? This must be Zade Galda's trading headquarters. He had this kind of stuff on his peddler's wagon!"

Fascinated, Rod kept looking at the strange assortment of gear. This could be Zade Galda's cabin, but there was no item here that would identify the bearded man.

"If we could just find something that he's tried to sell you," he said feverishly, "or something that I would recognize."

"I'm looking," replied Dolly, without taking her eyes off the mess of stuff that crammed every corner. "I'm looking, Rod, but I don't see any ribbon. I honestly don't see . . ."

"Wait!" Rod moved toward a wooden bench. In one corner near the wall, tucked under a piece of canvas where it hardly could be seen, was a small chest—about the size of the one Rod had watched the Indians give to Galda. It was not silver but dark green, and he thought as he drew near it that he was being a little foolish to get excited about it.

But his eyes jerked wide as he moved aside the canvas. There, on one side of the box was a face—brow and nose jutting out in the strange fashion of the silver chest.

A green box—and just like the silver one! He could not understand it.

"Dolly!" he called. "Look at this!" And when she too was standing before the chest, he said slowly, "This may be Galda's place, after all. This box is just like the other one he had, only it's green instead of silver. Do you suppose he had the silver one copied? Or are there lots of boxes like this?"

"I never saw one," mused Dolly, as she ran her fingers over the metal and traced the molded face. "Isn't it queer—like something from another land. Do you suppose," she looked at it closely and scratched it lightly with her fingernail, "do you suppose it might . . ." And then suddeny she shook Rod by the arm in excitement and pointed at the chest.

Where her nail had scraped the surface, a flake of green had peeled away, revealing a shiny spot beneath.

Rod stared. "It's been painted!"

"It's the silver box, Rod!" Dolly chanted exultantly. She flaked away another bit of the green paint, exposing more silver. "It's Galda's! Oh, I'm so glad we came to this place. Now General Hernandez can find him!"

"Maybe," replied Rod. He was lifting the lid of the chest. For a long time he had wondered what was inside it. Sometimes he had believed it was gold coins, another time he had guessed jewels. But he was unprepared for what he saw. There, half filling the box, lay a double handful of dark-brown twisted things.

Dolly, too, was staring in surprise at the contents of the box. "Well, of all things!" she said at last. "Roots!"

Chapter 15

Confiscated

"Soldiers! Much as you have performed, more remains
to be done; the enemy awaits you in fastnesses more
difficult than any you have yet penetrated. The government has adopted the only policy which can preserve
the Indians as a distinct and independent people. That
policy must be accomplished, and the Seminoles removed."

—From Order No. 203,
Major General Thomas S. Jesup,
1837

AND ROOTS they were. Rod scarcely could believe
that a box made of silver would contain anything so
ordinary as roots. He looked at them curiously, touched
one with a finger.

"They've been washed clean," he observed. "Maybe
they're used for some kind of medicine."

And suddenly remembrance struck through him as he
thought of Shakochee's root, the precious one that would
bring a person back "almost from death."

Could these be the same as the one his Indian friend
had given him? Rod fished deep into his pocket and

brought up the pea-size bit. Holding it against the roots in the chest, he tried to make a comparison.

"What is that?" asked Dolly.

He explained that Shakochee had given him the root and what it was for.

"It looks like these," Dolly observed. "Dark brown and smooth on the outside. The piece you have is too small to tell what shape it has been."

Rod nodded. "It's the same, I'm positive. The Indians thought they were paying Zade a lot when they gave him these. But he was only interested in the box."

"Maybe he planned to resell them to the Seminoles some day," remarked Dolly cannily. "It looks to me as if he never gave up hope of selling anything. Some of the stuff here is so badly broken it never could be mended. Either Galda is a master craftsman, or he's just a stingy man, who can't let go of anything."

"It's what you said last," Rod agreed, fingering the roots. "I wonder . . ." He paused, thinking deeply.

"Wonder what?" asked Dolly.

"I wonder if the chest's been here ever since Galda was arrested that first time."

"Probably has," surmised Dolly. "Who'd guess it was silver? With this paint it looks like tin."

"And that's just the way Galda wanted it to look."

"He's sharp," said Dolly. "I'm glad I didn't buy the hair ribbon—he'd have cheated me!"

Rod reached into the chest, picked out one of the hard

brown objects and examined it closely. A sudden longing to take the roots possessed him. Shakochee would value them greatly. Some day perhaps the two of them would meet again, and Rod could give his friend the contents of the box, to be passed among Shakochee's relatives and later to his children and his children's children.

The young scout was silent, then dropped the root reluctantly. "I'd like to own these. But I guess it's too soon. Galda might come back and miss them."

Dolly's face was grave under the shadow of her sunbonnet. "They don't belong to us," she reminded. "We'll have to get the government to confiscate them."

A sudden uneasiness moved Rod to lower the lid of the chest. "We'd better report to the general. If Zade comes back, they can pick him up and take him to the fort. And they'll want to question the other fellow, too."

"Yes, indeed, he . . ." Dolly's words died on her lips. She stood rigid, listening. From far off came the faint drum of a pony's hoofs.

Fear leaped through Rod. "It's him—let's hide!"

Dolly clutched his arm, her face so pale that the freckles stood out sharply. "We can't. There isn't any place." She looked wildly around. "No, Rod, we'd be caught. It's that man we saw before, I bet. Let me talk . . ."

She broke off as the tall half-breed stood in the doorway. At sight of the two young people he frowned darkly and his hand moved toward the knife at his belt.

To Rod's amazement, Dolly seemed to relax. She smiled her best company smile and pattered toward the man, exactly as if she were greeting one of the boys at the schoolhouse dance.

"How do you do, Mr. . . . ?" She skipped the name and went on hastily. "We were wondering if you wouldn't be back soon. The trader told us to come out here if we needed anything for our house in town. He wanted Mother to buy a pair of silver candlesticks, but I don't see them among your articles here."

"What you want?" asked the man suspiciously. His speech was even more broken than Galda's.

Dolly pushed back her sunbonnet and smiled again. "Why—the candlesticks. Mother sent me to tell Mr. Galda he could bring them in any time. I knew he wouldn't mind if we looked over his things."

The man stared searchingly at her. His voice was gruff. "Which candlestick? I see no candlestick."

Dolly glanced around the hut, unhurriedly, as if she hadn't seen it before. "I'm sure I don't know where they are, sir," she confessed. "I only know that when I told Mother I was coming out here for persimmons she said to stop and see the trader. She said . . ."

"Trader not here," the half-breed grunted. "Gone away." He motioned them toward the door. "Go."

"I hope you're not angry. I didn't mean any offense," prattled Dolly, wrinkling her brows as if she were terribly

upset, but walking swiftly toward the door. "Come, Rod."
And to the half-breed, "You can tell Mr. Galda to stop
and see us when he brings his wagon into town. Just tell
him the lady wants the silver candlesticks. He'll remember."

Together Rod and Dolly walked out the door and across
the clearing to their wagon. Rod gave Dolly a hasty help
up, and then sprang agilely to the driver's seat.

"Go slowly," cautioned Dolly in a whisper, her hands
shaking as she retied her sunbonnet strings. "We can't
look as if we're running away."

Rod tried to slow down. But it was agonizing to reach
out casually and take the whip, to touch it lightly to old
Maude's flank, to turn the mare in a wide circle and head
back along the trail, right past the cabin.

But Dolly talked on gaily about how the persimmons
ought to be extra sweet since last week's frost, and even
made him slow down while she pointed out a flock of
parakeets in the trees.

At last they were a mile past the cabin. Dolly ventured
a look back and saw that no one was coming. "Oh!" she
gasped. "Let's hurry, Rod."

"Not yet," he said cautiously. "That fellow may be
hiding back there where you can't see him. Sit tight
and we'll play out the whole game just the way you
started."

So they kept along the trail at old Maude's favorite

pace, a leisurely walk, while both of them wished fervently they were back in St. Augustine.

The detachment of soldiers sent out by General Hernandez took over Zade's cabin and arrested the half-breed. They toted the trader's property into camp and announced that anyone who had lost goods through theft could retrieve them with proper identification. Rod was not surprised to find that quite a number of things were returned immediately to their owners.

The government already had a claim against Zade for the powder and guns he had stolen, so the silver chest was auctioned off to the highest bidder and the money went to settle Zade's bill. General Hernandez, who had taken a liking to the strange little chest, bought it for a low figure, much less than its real value.

Although the half-breed could not be implicated in any of the thefts, he was threatened with a jail sentence if he didn't talk. He revealed that the trader had gone on a long trip south but would return. When, he refused to say. He seemed to be mortally afraid of the man.

As soon as Rod heard about the disposal of the chest, he hurried to General Hernandez's headquarters and asked if he could have some of the roots.

"Roots?" repeated the general vaguely. "Oh, you mean that old wood that was in it? We threw it away this morning."

"Threw it away!" repeated Rod, in anguish.

"Why, what's wrong? Is it worth anything?"

"It's medicine," Rod explained, "Indian medicine. I wanted it—that is, if you didn't."

"It may still be in the woodbox," offered the general helpfully. "I thought I'd burn it. Look over there and see."

Rod hurried to the big woodbox set near the stone fireplace. There, in the bottom, mixed up with pine splinters and a little sawdust, were his roots.

"All right, sir!" he assured the general. "They're here!"

"Take them and welcome!" The officer laughed. "They wouldn't have added much to the fire."

Rod picked them out carefully, tied them up with a rawhide thong, and took them back to his tent, where he stuck them under his army blanket. Later, he promised himself, he would take them home. If he never saw Shakochee again, his mother would have use for them. Or perhaps he would sometime have another Indian friend.

A week passed and word came from the south that Coacoochee had met Chief Arpeika near Fort Mellon and incited the hostile old warrior to take the warpath again.

The Indians once more retreated to their strongholds— dim hammocks surrounded by swamp water, islands rising from deep bogs, or any spot inaccessible to white armies. There they held angry talks and listened raptly to their councils of the dead.

Rod remembered the words of John Fox when he heard

about Coacoochee's escape. "Good-bye, peace" had more than come true.

Grimly General Jesup pressed forward with his campaign, which would send armies to all parts of the Territory: Colonel Zachary Taylor at Lake Kissimmee was to carry the attack south; Brigadier General Nelson would secure the frontier of Middle Florida; Colonel Persifer Smith was ordered to drive from the Caloosahatchie River to distant Cape Sable, General Hernandez to establish more southerly posts on the east coast, and General Eustis to strike south of Lake Monroe. Other forces also were in the field, scouring the Territory for Indians, and building new forts everywhere.

Rod's plans were to take a quick trip home before marching south with Colonel Taylor, who was in need of scouts. The central part of the state, where the columns would penetrate, was a wilderness familiar only to the Indians.

Although Rod regretted leaving Dolly and his two comrades, Hart and John Fox, he never once thought of refusing to accept service with Colonel Taylor. As he saw it, duty was duty. It was his business to go where he was needed.

As before, every Indian track was being followed, every band hunted down. General Jesup's policy of harassment, of killing cattle, burning Indian villages and crops, had discouraged the enemy and brought many important chiefs to surrender. With the main body now in Arkansas and many of their leaders there, with Osceola pining away in prison and Micanopy waiting patiently for emigration, there was only a desperate remnant to carry on the fight. The general had said they must be tracked to their haunts —the swamp-ringed island or isolated hammock—straight through the black swamp waters themselves.

Chapter 16

Phantom Enemy

"The difficulty is not to fight the enemy, but to find
him."
—Major General Thomas S. Jesup,
in an official report in 1837

SIX DAYS before Christmas Rod joined Colonel Taylor's men at Fort Gardiner on Lake Kissimmee and
marched south with them along the meandering Kissimmee River.

The colonel's forces had raided north as far as the Withlacoochee. They had captured a few Indians and scattered
others. Their orders now were to move toward the Territory's biggest lake—round Okeechobee, shallow and grown
with custard apple, still unknown to all but a few white
men.

Again it was the problem of finding the enemy. No lead
was considered too slight. The imprint of a moccasin or a
pony track called for pursuit. Detachments were sent out
to take even a single Indian.

It was not known if the Seminoles could be rallied again
for a full-scale battle.

Menacing as Colonel Taylor's army must have appeared to the enemy, the troops were a weary lot. They were not used to the languid climate of South Florida, nor to the three-sided sawgrass that slashed like sword blades and left a wound slow to heal. The miles of wilderness without a habitation awed them, and they grew to hate the sluggish Kissimmee looping through flat pinelands or losing itself in broad swamps.

Even the Florida volunteers, long accustomed to frontier hardships, were exhausted by pursuit of the elusive enemy.

Rod, who knew the Tampa area well, could only guess at what lay ahead, for there were few maps and no white men who had traveled this watery land. In wooded sections he scouted ahead, bringing back crude drawings to the colonel, who had them copied in ink and fitted into a chart that would represent the route.

As the woods gave way more and more to the rosette-like palms and broad stands of sawgrass, Rod's scouting trips became fewer, for now the eye could see all that lay ahead. Rod was glad. Like the others he preferred human company when his surroundings were strange. Besides he had found an old friend, Saul Sims, among the Florida volunteers commanded by Colonel Gentry. They marched side by side and often talked about home and Saul's fiancée in Tampa.

Rod smiled dourly as he padded along in the mud, listening to Saul's complaints that he'd better get back soon or Jane would be married to someone else. Although the young scout didn't consider Dolly a sweetheart, he often thought about her, wondering what she would say if she could see him now. His shirt was ingrained with dirt, his hair hung almost to his shoulders, and his soil-dark moccasins had been slashed ragged by the razor-edged grass.

Inside his hunting shirt was a note from her. Delivered to Rod at Fort Gardiner, it had long since taken on some of his grime and was dog-eared from much refolding.

Galda had not been captured, the note said, and there was no clue as to his whereabouts. The army seemed to have lost interest in the hunt, but Dolly promised she would watch for the trader herself.

The clean little bakery with its appetizing smells, luscious cream tarts, and friendly Dolly seemed a world away, almost as far as Rod's own home on the Hillsborough River. Often he dreamed of these two pleasant places at night, only to waken in the morning to the same silent comrades beside the serpentine river.

Saul began saying the army ought to quit. "Ought to go back home and let the Indians be."

"We can't do that," objected Rod. "We're in this war and we've got to finish it."

"It wasn't people like you and me that started it," grumbled Saul. "We can get along with Indians. You've even got a good friend that's an Indian."

"Sure have."

"Up in Walton County the Scotch Presbyterians that went in there lived right alongside the Uchee Indians for a long time without any trouble," continued Saul. "They treated them right, that's why."

Rod was silent.

"Now the Uchees are on the warpath," Saul concluded gloomily.

Still Rod didn't answer, and the Tampa volunteer looked at him with a piqued expression on his round face. "Isn't that true?"

"It's true," replied Rod wearily. "Only what can you do about it now?"

Saul wasn't satisfied. "What's the sense in dragging ourselves down here? There aren't any Indians around. Most of them been shipped west."

"Just enough warriors left to cause trouble."

"They won't do anything. They're through," scoffed Saul.

"Jumper's still out, and Alligator," Rod reminded. "So's Coacoochee. They're all in this part of the country. I heard somebody say the other day that the Prophet was down here, too."

"Prophet!" Saul spat out the name. "Nobody's scared of him. He stands back of the lines and dances, I've heard said, while the young men go in and get shot!"

Rod thought of Shakochee. Was his friend among these Seminoles and Miccosukies—fleeing south, penetrating the watery glades of lower Florida, where few men had lived before? Was he being herded like them into a smaller and smaller space, turning to fight back but always losing and retreating? Might he be one of the young men killed in battle?

He wished—if Shakochee was still alive—that the boy would come to terms with General Jesup and go west. For, distant and strange as Arkansas seemed, it offered a peaceful home.

The days slipped past monotonously. Then one night the Indian chief, Jumper, came in, surrendering himself and his band of sixty. They were dispatched with a guard to Fort Fraser.

Saul was happy. "It's that many more savages ready to ship," he rejoiced. "Now, if we can only smoke out the others!"

"It's not always that easy," remarked Rod, thinking of the battles he had been in.

Several nights later, Rod and Saul were roused from sleep and ordered to report to Colonel Taylor. The two dressed hastily and stalked through the darkness to the colonel's tent.

Inside, the officer was waiting for horses to be brought up. He explained their mission tersely. "Our advance battalion has sent word that Alligator's camp lies ahead. The chief and most of his warriors have gone somewhere, but the people want to be taken so they won't be forced to fight. Rod, you'll interpret, of course."

The night was cool, its sky ablaze with stars. The tepid atmosphere was like springtime and the air so softly clear that Rod could note a dozen odors. Mingling with the green scent of trampled grasses was the smell of the horses, and the aroma of smoke lingering in leather garments stole out into the darkness. Rod even could detect the oil on his own rifle.

Saul, riding beside him, pointed to a falling star. "Some folks say it means somebody died."

"Maybe there's going to be a battle."

"Maybe."

"You'd be glad to fight them and get it over, wouldn't you?"

"It's better than trailing these blasted savages and never finding them," admitted Saul.

"You sound as if you hate them."

"I do now. I didn't use to."

"What changed you?"

Saul reined in his horse and guided it around a swampy spot. "This long ride, I guess. I didn't hate Indians so bad, even when I started. I was like you, I just wanted peace."

"We all want that."

"But this country does funny things to a fellow," admitted Saul. "It's queer and different, not like farther north. It's like we was in enemy territory."

"It's that, all right," agreed Rod.

Saul wiped his forehead with his neckerchief. "Seems like there's getting to be more snakes and buzzards and 'gators the farther we go. I don't like it."

"You'll forget it all when the fighting begins."

"Will I?" worried Saul. "Sometimes I wonder. This lazy-like weather takes all the spunk out of a fellow."

Rod remembered that Saul had never been in a battle, and he tried to recall his own feelings that first day on the Withlacoochee. "You'll fight when the time's right," he assured him.

"Will I?" said Saul again, his voice low and strained. "This country's given me the fidgets. It even makes me wonder will I be yellow when the time comes."

Gradually the sky lightened and the stars dimmed along the eastern horizon. Colors began to show, the faint yellow of dawn on the river, the green of sawgrass, and finally the brown maple of Saul's gun butt.

Ahead of them a dark lump that had lain mysteriously against the sky began to reveal itself as a palm hammock. And as the morning brightened, Rod saw Indian huts within the shadows.

"Look—the camp!" he exclaimed.

Almost at the same instant, the colonel shouted orders to spur ahead and surround the Indians.

Rod and Saul gouged their horses into a gallop, and the whole detachment came thundering down upon the sleeping camp, spreading out and around the thatched dwellings until the inmates were trapped. No one tried to escape, and in a few moments an old man emerged, holding a white feather and crying out in Seminole that he wanted to speak to the commander.

The colonel and Rod rode toward him.

"We give up," the old fellow panted. "There are twenty-two of us. We surrender to the white army!"

The colonel barked orders to round up the Indians. Immediately the troops closed in, herded the twenty or so women and children into little groups and brought them before the officer.

"You have surrendered to Colonel Zachary Taylor," he told them, with Rod recasting his words into Seminole. "Obey my soldiers and no harm will come to you."

The old man he chose to question further. "Where is Alligator?"

"With the Miccosukies," said the old one, his wrinkles bunched together with anxiety.

"Where is the Miccosuki camp?"

The Indian hesitated, obviously torn between fear and the desire to answer. At last he said, "Across the Kissimmee. Twenty miles away."

"Twenty miles," repeated the colonel. Rod thought his eyes showed a certain hard satisfaction. "Is that where they will fight?"

"That is where."

Rod's heart beat fast at the words, and he saw the same excitement in the colonel's face. Indians—ready to fight. Nothing like that had happened all during this march. He could hardly believe it.

"Go to Alligator," said the colonel, "and tell him to meet me tomorrow at Kissimmee, where the trail crosses. We will wait there. If Alligator surrenders to us, we will protect him."

They watched the old man turn and walk slowly between the palms until his thin figure was out of sight.

The detachment waited for the main army to catch up, then continued the march until late that evening, when they encamped at the Kissimmee River crossing, as the colonel had promised.

Rod was anxious. Would Alligator surrender? The officer paced about uneasily.

After several days the messenger reappeared and came to the commander's tent. He was received brusquely.

"What did Alligator say?"

The old one's eyes were shifty. "Alligator wishes to meet you here, but he cannot come when you have said."

"He doesn't want to surrender," observed the colonel tartly. "Don't bother to translate that, Rod, but ask him if the Miccosukies are at the same camp."

Rod conveyed the message. The elderly man nodded. "They are at the same camp."

"Are they still waiting to fight?"

Again the man nodded. "They wait to fight."

"We will indulge them," said Colonel Taylor, a half-smile on his lips.

Rod's blood ran fast. At last, after all the marching, they had come to the big battle. He did not like war, nor did he face battles with elation. But if they had to be fought, he, like Saul Sims, wanted them to be fought and done.

Chapter 17

The Battle

"The most spectacular campaign was fought by Colonel Zachary Taylor, a young man still, who was to become Old Rough and Ready, hero of the Mexican War and the twelfth president."
—Marjory Stoneman Douglas
in *The Everglades: River of Grass*

IT WAS Christmas Day, sun-bright but dreary, like all the recent days of this march. The troops stood ready for battle.

Gentry's Volunteers were at the front to spearhead the attack. They were flanked by Morgan's Spies. Behind them was the infantry, fourth and sixth, which formed a second line. The regulars had orders to sustain the front-line fighters, or take over the battle if the volunteers broke.

Ahead lay a broad swamp, grown higher than a man's head with the sharp-bladed sawgrass. One could only guess at the depth of the black water. Beyond it a cypress hammock reared its leaf-naked branches.

It's just like Wahoo, Rod thought, as he stood among Gentry's men, waiting for orders. The swamp for us to cross, the Indians waiting in a hammock, picking us off as we advance. A crafty plan, designed to even up the odds.

No frontiersman would send troops across this swamp in the face of gunfire, he realized. But the army would, and he was a volunteer, fighting under an army colonel.

"Forward, march!"

The order rang along the line and the troops moved ahead. Rod took his first step into the water, felt soft muck rise over his moccasins. The ooze was soft here, and deep. Unless the ground firmed farther out, it would be a hard crossing.

Saul Sims strode beside Rod. He looked neither to right nor left, but Rod guessed his feelings—relief that the fighting had come at last and a deep, half-buried fear that he might be yellow. Only when the battle began would he know for sure.

With each step the water rose higher. It came to Rod's ankles, moved up to his calves, then his thighs. With one hand he held his rifle above the water. With the other he shortened the thong on his powder horn. He wondered if Colonel Taylor had expected a swamp this deep. They still hadn't reached the middle.

At halfway across, the water came almost to Rod's waist. The men were holding their guns and powder over their heads. But they were moving ahead, steadily preserving their line.

A sharp cry of "Yo-ho-hee!" rang from the hammock. It was repeated again and again, slapping through the cypress like the snarls of a rioting dog pack. Puffs of smoke began to blossom within the tree shadows, followed by the dull groan of rifles.

Rod paused behind a thick clump of sawgrass, picked his next shelter-clump and pushed quickly toward it. This sniping clearly was planned to throw fear into the white men. Not many would be killed, for the grass partially hid them and they were moving targets. The volley would come when they were closer.

To Rod's left, Sims was heading towad an open space. The young scout called out a warning: "They've cut the sawgrass. Stay away, Saul!"

Sims waded around.

The water became shallower. As its roily depths receded, the men moved faster, paced by Colonel Gentry. At two thirds of the way he shouted an order.

"Take cover!"

The men scattered to hide behind high-grass clumps. As they crouched there, awaiting the next order, Rod stared ahead into the twilight depths of the hammock. He saw bright shirts, red and blue turbans, and the flash of fringed leggings. Some of the warriors roosted high in the trees. Others hid behind the broad-boled cypresses, their rifles resting in notches that had been hacked out of the trunks.

He spotted a splash of saffron behind a sheaf of moss in a big tree. Aiming his rifle and sighting carefully, he waited until the order came to fire. As his gun roared, he saw the moss jerk. The saffron was gone. No other clue told him if his bullet had found its mark.

Again he poured powder into the muzzle, jammed in a patch-wrapped ball, and with his ramrod choked the whole charge down.

As at Wahoo, and in every battle he had fought, he found himself thinking of Indians as people. How had the Territory got into this war where men were forced to violate the sixth commandment? And how could things be changed for the better?

In a painful intuitive flash he saw that those who would choose peace must watch the actions of government as closely as they watch the deeds of their own lives. For what is begun must be finished, be it good or bad. Enough good men, actively opposed to the Treaty of Payne's Landing, could have changed or prevented it, and this battle might never have come about.

Through his head rang the Biblical words of Micah, as he had heard his father read them on Sundays: "What does the Lord require of you but to do justice . . . ?"

"Move ahead, men!"

Again Rod waded toward the hammock. The line was ragged, its soldiers coming from behind cover and striding forward in uneven ranks.

Gunfire spewed hotly from the cypress. Snipers' bullets slashed through the tall grass or whipped the surface of the swamp water. Still the volley had not come.

"Move ahead, men!"

Into the silence rolled a shout in Seminole. The thunder of the enemy's volley came at last. Leaden hail whistled out of the grove. Men fell, splashing into the shallows.

The volunteers were running hard, through the last clumps of sawgrass, pressing toward the hammock. The Seminole's rifles vanished, one by one, from the cypress notches. The depths of the forest flickered with retreating figures.

"Move ahead, men!" shouted Gentry. "Into the woods!"

Rod waded through the sawgrass onto higher ground. He wormed his way between the domelike roots of a cypress, stood sidewise against its bulbous trunk, and primed his gun for a second shot. Now there was no fear of death, no high-flown thoughts of justice. Only a heightened physical power and sharpened cunning.

Ahead of him an Indian stepped out from behind a tree to shoot. Rod fired. The man toppled backward. Rod did not pause to see if he was wounded or dead.

Men were falling everywhere. Rod kept going. Saul Sims was safe, too. He stood near by, jamming another ball into his rifle, aiming, firing, reloading again.

From the left came a cry: "Gentry's down! He's shot!"

Rod reloaded coolly. This time he fired at an Indian figure that ran squarely across his sight. The man stumbled, but kept his feet and disappeared in the woods.

The volunteers' fire was fading away. Rod glanced to his right. There was no one. To his left Sims still squinted along his rifle barrel. Where were the others?

Despair filled Rod as he guessed the answer. They had panicked. Without a leader, they had broken and turned back.

He glanced behind him. There came the blue of the army, advancing, straight and steady. The regulars were almost up to him. He would stay. Quickly he reloaded, primed, and sought for a new target within the hammock.

Ahead he saw Saul Sims on one knee, reloading behind a sapling stand overgrown with creeper. Poor cover, thought Rod. But before he could shout a warning, the creeper whipped sharply. Saul cried out as he fell.

Forgetting his own safety, Rod ran to him. Saul struggled to rise. The front of his shirt was wet with blood.

"Lie still!" ordered Rod.

He bent low and ripped open the shirt. A chest wound. Again Saul struggled to get up, tried to grip his gun.

"Lie down!" urged Rod. "You're hit, Saul! Lie still. I'll help you."

"I'm not scared."

Rod stared at his friend, understanding suddenly. Saul had been afraid. It had preyed on him. "Will I be yellow when the time comes?" he had said that night. Now the battle was in progress, he had fought well. He was proud. Even death couldn't scare him.

"You're hit pretty bad," Rod pleaded. "Hold still, so you won't bleed."

"I'm all right. Let me up."

"No, you aren't. Hold still. Hold still, I say."

He groped in Sims' haversack and drew out a bandage roll. The young private was quieter now, weak from loss of blood.

"That girl in Tampa'll sure be proud of you," said Rod as he tied the cloth tightly around the wound. "She'll always think of you as a real fighter."

Sims smiled faintly. "Have we beat them yet?"

"They're dropping back."

"Good."

Rod tied the bandage, turned Sims farther onto his back in a way he thought would check the blood flow. He wondered what else he should do. Hunt for the stretcher bearers? Try to take Sims in himself?

Saul settled it for him. "Go on ahead," he urged, "so the volunteers won't look shabby. I'll be picked up soon."

Rod gave Saul a comforting pat on the shoulder, took up his rifle again. "So long, fellow. I'll come past on my way back to make sure you got taken in."

"So long."

From the safety of a cypress ahead, Rod looked around

him. The fourth infantry had caught up, and as its men moved forward, he moved also.

It was slow going. Every inch of ground was stubbornly contested. Rod saw the army men dead on the ground but could not stop to help. Even those who fought on were bloody from their wounds. Blood stained the dark water of the bogs and made banners of the leafy undergrowth. Blood sceped from fallen bodies into red pools that sickened the sight.

Rod had made fun of the regulars—he and the other frontiersmen—said they weren't woods fighters. Said they exposed themselves foolishly. Now he was forced to admit they were dedicated men, brave and steady under fire, forming a hard core that would not be broken.

And the thought came, in a faraway, remote part of his mind, that their high honor, dearer even than life, was the kind to strive for at all times in every branch of government. For it seemed to him that only a small degree of such sacrifice by the nation's citizens would bring the much-desired peace.

Rod's hunting shirt was slashed from sawgrass and musket balls, but he had not been struck. One cheek leaked blood from a bullet burn, that was all.

Gradually the cypress hammock thinned. The foe was harder to find. The bleeding troops pressed forward, moving faster, running between leafless cypress trees, splashing through muck and water.

Just when it seemed there could be no end to the battle, the woods lightened and the men burst onto a white-sand beach of a broad lake.

"Okeechobee!" someone shouted exultantly. "Lake Okeechobee!"

The shallow lake stretched before them, round and serene in the late afternoon sun. Its wading birds had been frightened away by the noise of battle, and its fish had sought the shelter of deep places. But far off, Rod saw a crane take flight, its wings beating hard to catch the air currents.

Even this beach was not the end of Seminole resistance. To the left a puff of smoke bloomed from within the cypress. Then other puffs made the soldiers duck back to cover.

Rod and a handful of men plunged on fiercely, penetrating the woods. At first they ran unchallenged. Then came gunfire, two rifles spitting at them out of the brush. The group faltered and broke. As the firing increased, they began to retreat, sifting slowly back through the trees.

Rod, too, thought it time to go back. But as he halted, an Indian perched high in a tree emptied his rifle at the boy. The bullet spanked his sleeve.

Both scared and mad, he moved forward again to his tree shelter and hunted for his enemy in the treetops. At first he saw only the gaunt limbs of the cypress and the moss that dripped thickly from them. Then he spotted the Seminole, propped in a limb-crotch, reloading.

Rod raised his gun and aimed. When the sight lay directly over the fellow's heart, he tensed his hand to squeeze the trigger.

But something made him pause. That brown leg bracing the Indian against the limb, that moccasined foot, the slope of the shoulder—he knew them. And through his anger and fatigue flowed a cold, refreshing stream of memory.

Shakochee. It was he. This was the time of which both had spoken long ago, when one should catch the other in his gunsight and see, not an enemy, but an old friend.

Rod lowered his rifle. Although Shakochee had shot at him, he knew it was accidental, as surely as he knew he himself would not kill the Indian in the tree. He was glad the others had gone—they would be of a different mind.

He pursed his lips, gave the shrill squawk of the fly-up-the-creek and then the whippoorwill cry as he had heard it the night the Indians left Fort Brooke.

He waited. From the tree came an answering call—first the heron, then the whippoorwill.

Rod started from behind his shelter. He must tell Shakochee to go. There was no safety here. White troops, great numbers of them, were coming through to the beach. They would follow the Indians until the last one had vanished. Then they would search for their own dead and wounded.

Shakochee must follow his people, quickly, before it was too late.

As the white boy ran toward the high cypress, a rifle shot sounded. It came from deeper within the hammock, where saplings grew around a huge, lightning-blasted tree.

Rod dropped in his tracks and lay still. A terrible sickness spread through him. The sunlight deepened into shadow. The sounds of the forest faded slowly into silence.

Chapter 18

Work of the Root

"The villages of the Indians have all been destroyed
and their cattle, homes and other stock, with nearly
all their property, taken or destroyed."
> —Report by Major General Thomas S. Jesup
> to the Honorable J. R. Poinsett,
> Secretary of War

THE MAN with the twisted nose lowered his gun. A
deep satisfaction warmed his skinny body. His most
irritating enemy, his gadfly, was dead. And he could count
on that Indian in the tree to stick a knife in Rod Wheeler's
back before joining the fleeing Miccosukies.

Dimly, in the recesses of his mind, the man was curious
about the bird calls. They had seemed to mean something.
But against the fact that his bullet had struck Rod, such
details faded into unimportance.

Slowly he reloaded his gun, thinking with self-pity what
a long time he had spent in Indian camps since the night
of Coacoochee's escape. Half-starved, hunted, and lately a
victim of malaria, he had been afraid to show himself in the
settlements, for every report told him that the army was on
his trail.

The information had come to him piecemeal from rare news of the upper East Coast. Some of it had been brought by a Negro who had escaped his master and joined the Indians. And once, in the isolated cabin of a dead white man, he had found supplies wrapped in an old newspaper which offered a reward for word of Zade Galda's whereabouts.

Even the Indians feared and avoided him, for they knew he had angered the golden god. He had been forced to follow them from camp to camp, scraping remnants of spoiling meat from the beef carcasses they left, but keeping always out of their sight.

He stretched his legs and was angered at their weakness. For it was time now to run from the white troops coming through the wood. This nest of saplings at the foot of a blasted cypress had made a good hide-out during the battle. But when the soldiers came hunting for their dead he wanted to be gone.

In his pockets was a small store of jerky, which he had saved up with the idea of walking to the coast. There he hoped to find passage on a schooner sailing north. Although he had no money, he hoped yet to profit by the golden god. For it was his plan to sell a map showing the location of the idol. He had failed to find it in the muck and quicksand of the creek, but he felt certain it would again lure someone to the stream.

His eyes probed the cypress. What was going on over

there? Why didn't the Indian drop out of his tree and finish off Rod Wheeler? Soon the white troops would be tramping through to the lake and it would be too late.

Zade raised himself cautiously on one elbow and stuck his head above the concealing ferns. Relief came over him as he saw Rod still lying on the ground. But as the man's eyes found the tall cypress where the Indian roosted, a cold current of fear washed over him. There, leaning toward him, was the Seminole. The warrior's rifle was angled down toward Zade's hiding spot, and the fellow seemed to be sighting coldly his way.

Zz-ing!

Zade grunted at the stab of pain in his middle, doubled over. But not before he had glimpsed the face behind the gunsight. He knew that face. That trigger hand once had almost killed him.

In soundless panic he struggled to his feet, crashed through the shielding undergrowth of his shelter, and ran back into the forest. His one thought was to get away before the Indian reloaded. He hardly felt the gun wound. He forgot about the white soldiers. Wildly he lurched through looping creeper vines, dodged tree trunks, and splashed through muddy water.

He ran for almost half a mile before weakness began to overtake him. It came first as a hard thumping of the heart, then a slowing of his run. At last it was a weight that he could no longer carry.

He waded into a miry stretch. The mud sucked hungrily at his feet, holding him back. He staggered, caught himself, and went on.

Halfway across the watery spot, his feet refused to move ahead. Their heaviness was unbearable. His head swam.

Hastily he looked around. He must not fall here. He would drown. No one would know that he was gone.

With all his remaining strength he kept on. Mists of darkness drifted between the trees. He fixed his eyes on one big cypress ahead, rooted half in the swamp, half out. If only he could reach it. He could hang onto it and creep up the bank.

He stumbled, fell, almost at the foot of the great tree, clutched at its arching roots. Blood from his wound stained the swamp water.

He tried to call, but his voice had no strength and was suddenly choked.

Dimly he heard noises deeper in the forest. Orders from an officer, the brisk, "Yes, sir," of a soldier. The voices grew louder. Footsteps brushed along the edge of the pool.

Zade made no sound as the men drew him out of the water and laid him on a stretcher.

Although Shakochee reloaded swiftly, intending to kill Zade Galda with his second shot, he saw as he raised his gun that it was too late. The fellow was out of sight. He could hear him crashing through the undergrowth, getting farther away every minute.

No use waiting, the Indian reasoned. No use trying to catch him, either—for there was Rod to care for.

He slid hastily down the tree and ran to the white boy. The stillness of the body frightened him. When he was close he saw a bullet hole in the back of Rod's hunting shirt.

A deep fear seized the warrior. This was a bad hurt. This time Rod would be lucky to live.

For an instant he stood over the body, wondering what he should do. White soldiers would take care of Rod if they knew where to find him. Perhaps it would be wise to give a war whoop and draw them to this section of the forest. He himself still could get away.

But Shakochee did not move, nor shout "Yo-ho-hee!" For in his pocket he had a piece of the magic root. Although his white friend, too, had a bit of the root, he could not move or speak, and so could not make himself well.

With a hasty glance around, the Indian picked Rod up by the shoulders and dragged him toward the blasted tree where Galda had hid.

From inside the hiding spot, he straightened the ferns that had been mashed down and drew a straggling bit of moss between himself and the forest. He did not waste time uncovering Rod's wound, nor do anything but turn the bullet hole upward as he had seen white men do.

Rod groaned and the Indian spoke to him: "It is I, Shakochee. Can you hear me?"

The scout opened his eyes, fixed them on the young

warrior. Pleased, the Indian reached into his pocket and drew out the root. With his hunting knife he whittled off a bit and began to macerate a tiny piece by pounding it with the knife handle against the butt of his rifle.

When he had finished, he tried to put the shred into Rod's mouth, but the white boy raised his hand to talk.

"Go," he said, his voice stronger and his eyes earnest. "The men will find me."

Shakochee shook his head stubbornly. "Not until you have had the root. They have no root. They cannot cure."

Again he offered the bit of mashed root. Rod took it into his mouth this time and chewed it.

"Go now," he said.

"It is late," observed Shakochee. "The dark is coming. No one will find us. Before morning I will go. I will be safe here."

Rod fell asleep soon. Shakochee sat beside him. When the moon rose and illumined the gaunt, moss-draped cypresses, the Indian rose, looked warily around him, and at last threaded his soft-footed way to the lake. There he drank deeply. He brought water and gave it to Rod when he woke.

"Are you better?" he asked.

"Yes."

"The root will make you well, Luckmaker," Shakochee told him confidently. "Twice it has cured me—once at the Place of the Dead and again at Fort Mellon. Soon you will feel stronger."

"Go, Shakochee," said Rod. "I'll be all right."

"I will stay a little longer."

Rod spoke again when the bright ball of Venus showed through the saplings. "Go now. The sun's almost up."

"I will stay."

"No," protested Rod, his voice strong. "I'm well. Your root has cured me."

Shakochee's face glowed. "The root always cures," he assured Rod. "There is only one danger. One must walk easily when he gets up, so the blood will not come again."

Then he remembered another most important thing which must be explained. "It was not I who shot you," he said earnestly. "I fired once. I did not know. I saw only that you were a white soldier. Perhaps the gods sent my bullet wide of its mark. But this ball, the one that hurts you now, came from Zade Galda, the Spaniard."

"Galda!" repeated Rod, dazed.

"Yes," said Shakochee emphatically. "His nose is twisted where I shot him, but I knew him anyway. He was hiding here—in this exact spot."

"Where did he go?" asked Rod.

Shakochee looked downward as if he were suddenly ashamed. "I fired at him but he did not fall."

"He has nine lives," commented Rod bitterly, "and none of them any good. But never mind, Shakochee. He'll pay sometime."

"It is so," agreed Shakochee, pleased that his friend and he thought so much alike.

Rod stiffened suddenly, lifted his head. "I hear someone. Go, Shakochee. Go quickly. Thanks for the root. Don't worry about me. I'm well."

Shakochee, too, was listening. From the shore of the lake, now glistening faintly with reflections of the rising sun, came the sound of tramping boots.

Shakochee jumped to his feet and peered through the trees. There, not more than a hundred feet away, were men of the United States Army, coming to look for their wounded.

The Indian turned sharply and ran in the opposite direction, trying to make his feet light as those of the black panther. Behind him he heard the soldiers call out, order him to halt. But he did not stop. A rifle sounded. A bullet zzinged past him, snipping off a tree twig. A second ball whipped harmlessly against his clothing.

He felt as if he were running on clouds. These men were trying to kill him, yet he did not care too much. Life was filled with danger, and he thought lightly of death. If he were wounded, the root would cure him. If he were dead, he would travel into the world beyond life.

He had done a good thing—he had cured his friend Luckmaker. The deed lent a new luster to his personal honor.

Beneath his pride was the rekindled love for his fellow men, which he always felt when he met Luckmaker and talked with him for a while. White men were not all bad, as the Seminoles and Miccosukies said. Some were good. He knew one. And so there was hope—for himself and all the others who clung to their native lands in the face of gunfire and marching armies.

Yes, no matter what happened, he had known Luckmaker. It would make a difference to him always.

Rod called as loudly as he could. "Soldier, here!" He wanted help, but he also wanted to divert the men from chasing Shakochee.

"Where are you?" came the answer.

"Near the blasted tree."

In a moment a tall soldier stood over him. Rod had never seen him before, but he wore the uniform of the infantry. "Did he shoot you?" he asked excitedly. "I tried to get him, but I missed."

"No—he didn't hurt me," Rod said slowly, with a deep breath of relief. "Here, give me a hand. I think I can walk."

The soldier helped Rod to his feet. With one hand on a sapling, the boy decided he didn't feel bad at all. He thought with a glow of Shakochee's root. There really must be something to it.

In the same instant he spied the rest of the root almost at his feet. Still holding hard to the young tree, Rod reached down and grasped it. Without a word he dropped it into his pocket.

"Can you make it?" asked the soldier kindly. "We have some stretchers made of hides that we found in the Indian camp. Want me to get one?"

"I can walk," said Rod stubbornly. He took a slow step,

then another. "I feel pretty good. Bring my gun, will you?"

He walked out of the shelter and stood alone. The soldier handed him his rifle, and he found he could carry it.

He remembered what Shakochee had said: "Walk easily, so the blood will not come again."

One hand stayed in his shirt pocket, fingering the bit of root. Shakochee had cherished that root. He would grieve over its loss. Somehow Rod must manage to return it to him.

Chapter 19

Going Home

"My decided opinion is that unless immediate emigration be abandoned, the war will continue for years to come and at constantly increasing cost."
—Major General Thomas S. Jesup
in a report made
near the close of his service in Florida

"TELL YOUR mother I made this fruitcake last November, and it's just right to begin eating," said Mrs. James as she tucked a solid little parcel under Rod's arm. "And tell her I'm grateful for the medicine she sent me. My wrist hardly ever pains me now."

"I'll do that, ma'am," promised Rod.

He gazed at the ragged flames of the dying wood fire in the James' living room. The old sofa, the oil paintings, and the familiar cream-tart desserts he'd had for supper had given him a twinge of homesickness almost as bad as the yearning he felt for the Hillsborough farm. Now that it was time to go, he hated to say good-bye.

"Tell your mother that Mrs. James' fruitcake is as fa-

mous as your medicine," put in Dolly, "and sometimes I
think it cures just as many things."

Mrs. James laughed. "It depends on your age, Dolly."

"Will you be planting cotton?" asked Dolly as Rod
moved toward the door.

He nodded. "And other things, I guess." It was almost
March and he knew his father would be putting in cotton
and corn and probably sweet potatoes. Although the scar
in Rod's back still was red, the ball had been removed, and
he felt as strong as before. He wanted to get a plow in his
hands, and a hoe, and to see the cotton sprouting and the
corn's green spears knifing through the black soil along the
river.

Hart was traveling with him. The two of them had managed to round up a horse apiece, and early in the morning
they were starting the long trip across the Territory.

They would leave Zade Galda in old Fort Marion, where
he occupied a casemate much like the one that had housed
Coacoochee. The Spaniard's original sentence had been
lengthened to forty years, for his part in aiding the Indian
leader, and it looked as if death might come before he was
free again.

Even if Galda gained strength—for his wound and fevers
had left him ailing—there was little chance for his escape.
The prison was now so closely guarded that even a lizard
sunning itself on the coquina walls did not go unnoticed.

The Seminole war still went on, and General Jesup's

numerous small armies still carried out their assignments, capturing Indians and sometimes fighting. But the warriors had been driven far to the south, and the remnant that now resisted was deep in the watery Everglades. To keep them from returning to the good lands, a line of forts had been built across the southern part of the peninsula.

The battle of Lake Okeechobee had been considered a great victory for the whites. Chief Arpeika had fled, along with the Prophet, leaving only Coacoochee and Alligator to carry on the fight. Thus the last organized Indian resistance had failed.

The settlers were building again—cabins, barns, bridges. Even the bigger plantations were repairing their thatched slave huts, and the fields were filled with slaves planting cotton.

Rod absently patted the fruitcake under his arm. A funny load he would be taking in his saddlebags—fruitcake and roots. For he still had the roots from the silver box. Perhaps, some day, he could get in touch with Shakochee. Just how it could be done remained a mystery, for there were no more "friendly Indians" to carry messages, and no Seminole slaves who dared show their faces outside the swamplands.

"Good-bye, Dolly." He shook her hand and looked for a long moment into her blue eyes. Would she be like Saul Sims' girl, who had married another man before Saul got out of the hospital and back to Tampa? Rod didn't think so. He believed Dolly and he would grow up together, even though the whole width of Florida separated them. Some day he would come back and find her here at the bakery, just the same as she was now, only older and taller maybe, and looking more grown-up, like a woman.

"Good-bye, Rod."

The boy looked away in sudden embarrassment as he saw tears in her eyes. "I'll write you a letter," he said suddenly.

The remark made her laugh. "If you do, it'll be the first one," she reminded him. "You've never written me a letter, you know."

"Haven't I?" It was surprising news to Rod. But as he thought back, he realized she was right. Any letters—and there hadn't been more than two or three—had come from Dolly to him.

"I'll do better," he promised. "Good-bye, Mrs. James."

"Come back to see us," the woman urged warmly. "And plan to stay with us next time. You're always welcome, Rod."

"Thank you, ma'am."

Rod opened the heavy door and walked toward the stair. "Good-bye," he said again. It was sad how little a person could convey to others with the English language. He had lots to say, yet he had only told them "Good-bye."

He walked down the stairs to the street, where he caught the sharp breeze from Matanzas Bay. Now that it's rained, it'll be turning cold, he thought. Good weather for the trail.

As he headed toward the room he and Hart shared, he thought again about home and his father and mother and two brothers. They'd be needing him. High time he got back.

"High time," he said aloud to the gusty wind.